MILTON: WORSHIP

A CLUB XXX NOVEL: BOOK SEVEN

LYDIA GOODFELLOW

LYDIA GOODFELLOW

Betty,
Enjoy the read.
Lydia Goodfellow

ALSO BY LYDIA GOODFELLOW

CLUB **XXX**

Worship

Reign

Worship

Worship By Lydia Goodfellow

Copyright © 2020 by Lydia Goodfellow
All rights reserved.

No part of this publication may be reproduced, distributed, or transmitted in any form or by any means, including photocopying, recording, or other electronic or mechanical methods, without the prior written permission of the author.

This is a work of fiction. Names, characters, businesses, places, events and incidents are either the products of the author's imagination or used in a fictitious manner. Any resemblance to actual persons, living or dead, or actual events is purely coincidental.

Editing by Micky Reed
Cover Design and Interior Formatting by Charity Chimni
Proofreading by Charity Chimni

TRIGGER WARNING

Please keep in mind that this story includes dark, graphic and explicit content matter that is not suitable for readers under the age of 18—or for readers who are uncomfortable with the following subject matter: explicit sex, mentions of sexual abuse, mentions of child abuse, graphic depictions of violence, and mentions of self-harm.

CLUB XXX

Welcome to Club XXX. While this is book 7 in the series, it is book one of Milton's story. This story can be read as a standalone without reading the first Club XXX books. The timeline for book 7 coincides with Book 1, Maxim: Submit.

ACKNOWLEDGMENTS

To Rob, thank you for putting up with my craziness and for telling me to go for it when I thought I wasn't good enough. For being there when my days were dark. I love you.

My babies, Aiden, Ryan, and Aria, I love you so much it hurts. This is all for you.

My fellow Irish woman, Keeva. Who would I be without you? Clearly running naked through the hills of Ireland. Thank you for believing in me, for being my friend, and keeping me sane all these years. I love you and can't wait until you share your writing with the world.

Nikki, my fellow dark writer who I love dearly, I simply couldn't imagine doing this without you. You've held my hand through this entire process and I couldn't be more grateful for all you've done. I can't wait to create more from this twisted world we've created.

Charity, you're like my fairy Godmother. You've come from nowhere, banished my anxiety and made anything I need happen. It really is like you're magic. Thank you.

To mum, dad and Ollie, I DID IT!!!!

Special shoutouts to my amazing aunt Janita, my best friend, Steph and wife Lucy. Life without you in it wouldn't be life at all. I love you, miss you, and so grateful to have you in my life.

To the rest of my family and wonderful friends, thank you so much for all the support. While I'm nervous about you reading this, let's just take a minute and admit we're all insane too, okay?

My readers, I hope you enjoy the first of many books to come. Dark souls unite!

CHAPTER ONE

Fair Haven City. Hell on Earth. A maggot-infested shell of depravity and a jungle of tall, cutthroat buildings shaded in black. As I breathe in, a phantom stench of fumes lingers beneath my nose, despite being in a room fragrant with flowers. As if the bitterness lacing my tongue and grit clinging to my skin will never erase from the days I lived and breathed the slums of it.

"Fair Haven. A place where no one sleeps. Not even the dead," I say, more to myself than anyone else.

But I do have a listener, and she moves behind me, emitting a breath loud enough to let me know she disagrees. "What do you mean by that?"

Allowing a few seconds of silence to linger, I finally face her. Sat on a high-backed chair, Dr. Ashley Rogue holds a notepad in one hand and a pen in the other. As she watches me, I know she already has me pegged as some spoiled teenage bitch begging for attention. Dr. Rogue is new here—came from Harvard a few months back, believing she can make a difference. Something they all believe at first. That is until they realize that's not how the world works. It's not how *Fair Haven* works. Black eventually seeps in and rots, and Ashley Rogue is already decaying.

"You will understand one day." It's a vague reply, and I'm aware she hates it. When I talk in riddles and never give a straight answer. Not anymore. Like clockwork, her forehead creases, and I know I've gotten to her.

Moving away from the window, I sit on the stereotypical couch, pulling my knees to my chest. I stare at her, and all she can do is look back.

When her gaze eventually averts back to her notes, my eyes roll. She can never look for long. As if she can't bear to see the truth screaming in my eyes. I am easier than most girls here are to read, knowing the visible scars on my skin paint a grisly picture of the life I've come from. Something that would make her platinum straight hair turn to frizz.

Instead, she writes something new. A lie. *Whatever.* I no longer care. Leaning my head back against the cushion, I look at a painting on the wall, something I always do whenever I'm here. It's supposed to be a bright, sunny piece of a young girl in a pretty yellow dress swinging from a tree. But the strokes of acrylic mar into something else. "Are you looking forward to staying with your mother—"

"*Gabriella.*" I cut in sharply. "It's Gabriella."

Her professional mask slips, and I know it's because she thinks I'm disrespectful for calling my mother by her name. It doesn't take a genius to work out that she's taken it personally. If I didn't know any better, I'd say it seems my dearest *mother* has already gotten to Dr. Rogue.

After all, Gabriella's most extraordinary power is corruption.

"May I ask why you call your mother by her first name?" I don't reply, and her eye twitches with annoyance. "She's looking forward to seeing you. She calls every day to check on your progress."

I bet.

Turning back to the picture, it's changed, just how it always does. The little girl isn't alone. Someone lurks behind the tree, another watching from afar. People who shouldn't be watching little girls...

"Heidi." Worry, at least I think that's what she's going for, furrows her brow. "I have to be honest with you. You aren't making progress. You refuse to talk about what really happened, and I fear it's hindering you from getting better. Please talk about it. I promise it will help."

She says this every week. Talk. Try. *Promise.* Talking will make it *all* better and magically go away. Yet the moment I tried when I first got here, Gabriella made it her mission to make sure everyone working here knew what a compulsive liar I was. That I enjoyed making terrible things up for attention.

Whatever I say won't be believed, and so I say nothing. And like always, Dr. Ashley Rogue sighs with disappointment, writes it down in her notes, and prescribes me something new to shove down my throat. Something I hope to fucking choke on.

"Ashley says you're not trying," Gabriella says, tone pissy and impatient. "Why the hell aren't you?"

Ashley. They're on a first-name basis now.

I don't know why Gabriella bothers ever asking, seeing as the public's sympathy has upped her book sales. While she wants me out of the way, we both know she would prefer if I kept my mouth shut about all the things that pull her away from the *mother of the year* title. I'm not delusional enough to believe she actually wants to *bond* with me during these times she comes to pick me up.

One day a week out of Stonehill is nothing but a photoshoot. A ploy motivated by greed. Being photographed taking her *psycho* daughter out and about makes her seem like the best mom in the world. When, really, she appeared on TV to promote her shitty books while I was in the hospital having my stomach pumped and a dead fetus scraped from my womb, even though she knew.

She knew…and she still didn't come.

Instead, her husband was quick to make all the bad things go away. He put me in Stonehill, sectioned under the watchful eyes of doctors and nurses, spouting lie after lie.

We had no idea she would do this.

This was a terrible shock to us all.

Stonehill is a secluded building on the other side of Crowe Park, the city a backdrop from its barred windows. The entire land is surrounded by electrical fences, the entrance heavily guarded with twenty-four-hour security. The building, tan-bricked and charming, boasts an illusion of a safe, nurturing place for young women haunted by their own demons. But it's nothing more than a glorified prison.

"Are you even listening to me, Heidi?" Gabriella demands, snapping me from my thoughts. "It's like I'm talking to a brick wall."

"Sure. I'm listening." She will only keep going on at me until I say something.

"You're incredibly difficult," she mumbles, and I peek a glance at her. At the stranger, I call a mother in my head, my subconscious never taking a hint. "You better not embarrass me today. I *mean* it."

Gabriella Lowden is beautiful and ugly. With her radiant skin, glamorous blond locks, and dressed in nothing but the finest, she's dripping in diamonds from her *beloved*. A matching set more than likely worth thousands of dollars. But on the inside... well, let's just say her blood runs black, not red.

Sucking Lawrence's dick years ago when she was still with my father made her who she is today. Fair Haven Times Bestseller of several books, including her very own autobiography. It conveniently leaves out her life before Lawrence and his riches. However, it does, of course, feature her troubling relationship with me. If that weren't enough, she is also co-founder of her own successful food brand, *Desired Foods*, an active charity contributor, and women's envy across the country.

Blah, blah, blah.

Embarrassing her is tempting, but I know I must behave. We're on our way to brunch with my stepsister, Elise, and while I'd rather chew off my arm than go, I have to be a good girl if I want more television time in my room.

Hiding the smile stretching over my lips, I point my gaze back out of the window and watch the world whizz by, satisfied that I got under her skin just a tiny bit.

We park outside a fancy restaurant moments later. A pearl, demure building that probably serves overpriced bits of food like every other swanky place Gabriella drags me to. Something she calls a treat in front of people, yet I'm waiting for it to feel like something other than torture.

The valet takes the car, and I reluctantly follow her inside. Elise is waiting for us as we walk through a set of glass doors. Wearing an elegant shirt, dressy pants, and stilettos, my older stepsister beams and waves excitedly.

"Elise, my darling!" Once she's near, Gabriella pulls her into an embrace. "Lovely to see you."

"I know, I'm sorry. I've been so busy with work. It's been too long." Elise's smile grows when she sees me in the background. "It's great to see you, Heidi. Beautiful, as ever."

Bowing my head, my face sears with heat. "Um…thanks."

I would love to say the smile painting her lips is forced. That she's just as arrogant and mean as her father, but it's not true. Despite not being blood-related, she's always tried to get to know me over the years. Tried to bond with the notion that we're real sisters.

I *have* a sister, and I don't want another one.

"Are you well?" Gabriella asks as we take a seat at a round glass table.

"I am. There's so much to tell you. But first, did you hear the latest?" They both dive into gossip—today's victim, an actress. She was caught cheating on her husband with her latest movie director. Gabriella expresses her disgust like she's in any position to be a critical bitch, and Elise agrees, thinking it unfathomable. Who says *unfathomable*?

With my hand resting under my chin and watching them both, my boredom grows by the minute. Being here with them is *so* painful that I itch for the outside. For freedom. *Air*.

Celebrity gossip and fashion aren't interesting topics, given that all I have to my name are the plainest cotton panties provided by

Stonehill. No expensive lace or silk. I'm not sure they're even real cotton.

"How is the publicity for the new book coming along?" Elise asks, changing the subject swiftly, which Gabriella must love, given that it's all about her.

"Busy, but amazing," she gushes. "I'll be going on the radio in a few weeks, and Naomi Wallas wants me on her talk show. Can you believe that?"

"That's amazing news. Anyone would be lucky to get a chance to sit and talk with you. I mean, I barely get to see my author stepmother these days."

"Nonsense, I always have time for you." I snort, which earns me a nudge under the table with her foot. But I can't help it, wondering if Elise would be as in awe if she knew Gabriella hired a ghostwriter.

Not that anyone ever believes me.

A little while later, as their voices drone on, I find myself staring at Elise, always holding a fascination for the lucky ones in this city and what makes them free and untouchable. I know the answer, of course. The only thing that makes the world tick —*money*.

Elise has a rich daddy to keep the monsters away. Although Lawrence married my mother, he made it clear over the years that he was never going to step into the role of being my father. And my own father didn't keep the monsters away. He fed me to them.

"What do you think of the fall and winter collections for this year, Heidi?" I blink, realizing I've done it again—drifted off into my own thoughts.

What are they talking about now? Oh, yeah, fashion.

"I don't really follow," I mumble, hating that she's talking to me. "I just wear whatever."

"You mean you wear what you've been *given?*" Gabriella pipes in, amusement peppering her tone.

Leaning back in my chair, shame prickles, like thorns stabbing my skin as I glance down at my outfit. I'm wearing Elise's hand-me-downs, dark blue jeans, a floral top I don't like, and a pink hoodie.

Stonehill has us all wear gray buttoned tunics and matching pants while we're there. But Gabriella makes me change before she takes me out, always bringing Elise's old clothes from the time she lived with them.

Elise smiles timidly, cheeks staining pink, and quickly changes the subject. Maybe because she's watching me gripping the butter knife so damn tightly.

"I have news," she announces after the waiter serves us plates of grass. I hadn't noticed him come over to take our orders.

"Oh?" Gabriella's eyebrows rise in wonder.

"Yes, there is a reason I wanted to meet with you both. You'll never believe it, but Scott proposed!" Lifting her hand, she shows off a massive rock sparkling on her finger, something I realize she hid well by keeping her hand under the table.

"Oh! Elise!" Gabriella grabs her hand to take a closer look. "I never thought he'd do it. Congratulations!"

"Neither did I. But Scott *finally* did in front of his family after Sunday dinner. He was such a sweetheart—got down on one knee and said how much he can't wait to spend the rest of his life with me."

"What a gentleman. I'm delighted for you. A lovely bit of news," Gabriella gushes. "Does your father know?"

"He does, of course, since Scott asked his permission. Daddy was going to tell you yesterday, but I wanted to tell you in person myself. We want it in the summertime and are already searching for a venue. We could use your expertise."

"Of course." Gabriella places her hand on her chest, flattered that she's being asked. "I would be honored. And I believe I have the perfect place in mind."

Abandoning the rabbit food, I make my way out onto the veranda that's not far from our table. They don't notice I've left, too busy discussing wedding plans with the *fantastic* Scott Link.

Leaning against the railing, I breathe in the crisp, autumn air. It's then that a single golden leaf blows off a tree nearby and dances in the air, eventually landing beside me. Picking it up, I observe its undamaged exterior. Beautiful. Perfect.

It shouldn't have left the tree.

Crumbling it in my hand, it breaks into tiny pieces, and when I open my palm, the wind carries it away. Forever broken. Because nothing can stay whole in this city. I know that better than anyone.

CHAPTER TWO

After brunch, Gabriella calls her driver to pick me up. She has an appointment to get her monthly dose of Botox, and I'm glad because it means I won't have to see her for the duration of my visit.

Now, her home isn't what we used to live in—a run-down, two-bedroom shithole situated in Horn Hill. This posh pad is far from what Gabriella used to have.

Used to *be.*

When I was younger, I don't recall a time when she wasn't obsessed over mansions, the rich, and their extraordinary lives. She often had arguments with Dad—never happy with what she had. That he couldn't provide everything she desired and deserved with his menial factory job.

After a while, he stopped listening, turning to alcohol to dull the ache. Then my sister, Nicole, stopped listening too, bored by her antics. That was when she enlisted me to be her new audience, and I was more than happy to be.

I'd sit for hours while she talked about her dreams and hopes of one day being proud of her achievements. It's funny that I once idolized her. Whenever she described the life we were going to have when we moved, I'd get excited. Like her, I didn't want to be stuck in Horn Hill—a scary place where all society's rejects breed. Where crime is rife, and the death rate is high.

But all those hopes and dreams were demolished the day she got a job at an insurance company as Mr. Lawrence Lowden's *personal* secretary. With Dad guzzling every drop of money he earned, desperation pushed Gabriella to apply to every job in the *Fair Haven Independent* just to keep food on the table. She wasn't expecting an interview when she applied for the position, but it surprised us when the call came.

She left school when she was fifteen and had no qualifications. At least, none to be a secretary. However, with his wife on her deathbed, Lawrence hired my mother because his dick got hard when he laid eyes on her.

She was even more stunning back then, before the enhancements and wealth. A sensual body Dad used to adore more than his nightly bottle of whiskey. Natural womanly curves and sultry brown eyes no man could ever look away from.

And Lawrence certainly didn't.

Gabriella didn't teach me many things, but there is one lesson I will never forget. That there is nothing, anyone wouldn't do for money. Even if it means destroying the people you love.

A Mediterranean-style stucco with two upstairs balconies stands before me. A home with too many rooms and breaching security guidelines with its large open windows, showcasing smooth marble floors, and modern furniture inside. A house that matches those mansions she used to drool over.

Letting myself in, I go upstairs to Elise's old bedroom. I know by the silence that greets me that I'm the only one here, except the security guard and housemaid, who seldom show their faces.

The only luxury of staying the night in this ridiculous place is swimming in the indoor pool. With that in mind, I pull out one of Elise's old bathing suits from the wardrobe. A pink one that has seen better days.

Shrugging off my hoodie and tossing it on the floor, I sit on the bed and undo the laces on my sneakers. As I reach to pull them off, my elbow slams against something hard behind me.

When I glance over my shoulder, my blood runs cold when my eyes land on a black object. A box, small enough for me not to have noticed on my way in, sits right there. Yet I *should* have seen it, as it's not just any ordinary box.

It's a coffin. My baby's coffin sits upon the once-white sheets, now dirtied from freshly *disturbed* soil.

Swallowing is impossible. The lump in my throat refuses to dislodge. Maybe I've lost the ability to breathe altogether. The only thought that comes to mind is that *he's* been here. He's been in this house, this room.

Seeing a black envelope on top of the lid, daring to be read, I snatch it from the coffin and stumble back from the bed, hands trembling as I rip open the paper and pull out a piece of card. Written in capital letters in blood-red ink, I almost bowl over and vomit up brunch as I read the words.

WE'RE COMING FOR YOU.

Squeezing the note in my fist, I close my eyes. There's wetness on my face, tears for a coffin that shouldn't be here. A reminder of the baby I lost. *My* baby.

Of course, the coffin is only symbolic. The only decent thing Gabriella's husband ever did for me because I'd been so distraught and begged him. I'd only been seven weeks, and I hadn't known. I didn't think it was there, inside of me, but that's no excuse. I killed my baby.

My knees give way. I'm on the ground before I'm aware of the hard surface under my butt. I crawl backward, putting as much distance from the terrible things I've done, envisioning the lid on the coffin opening and something coming out of it to drag me to hell. But there's no escaping, just like there's no getting away from *him*.

Didn't he always tell me he'd come for me? It was only a matter of time.

I let out a cry—a scream. I want my baby back, but not like this, *never* like this.

Cold reality sets in and turns my blood to ice. The man from my nightmares didn't think twice about ripping our baby from the ground because that's what he does. And he's not finished. Not by a long shot.

I don't remember arriving back in Stonehill the following morning. Having not slept, I don't recall being dropped off, going to my room, or a nurse coming to get me for an emergency session with Dr. Rogue.

"What happened?" she asks, hitting the tip of her pen off the notepad, waiting for my answer. "Was it another nightmare?"

I stare past her, at the painting on the wall, not in the mood to talk. Especially not to someone who thinks I'm lying. Once again, the picture has changed into something terrible. The little girl on the swing is now on the floor crying. Her pretty dress is ripped, panties tangled around her ankles. Bleeding and crying and screaming for her mommy. The salty taste of her tears is in my mouth—her suffering, my suffering. Because I once was her. I was that girl.

"Heidi," she continues, and I want to ram that stupid pen down her throat, especially as her eyes study me, watching me so closely for something. *Anything* to use against me. "Your mother said you had an episode?"

I don't know what I find more annoying. That Gabriella called it an episode after discovering me on the bedroom floor with my dead baby's coffin on the bed, or that Dr. Rogue *insists* on calling this woman my mother.

Mother called Lawrence to make it all go away. The coffin was taken back to the graveyard in a private car; the driver paid to keep his mouth shut. Then, after swallowing another pill while Lawrence had his back turned, she went to bed sobbing, leaving him to clean up the rest of the mess.

He was angry. Confused.

I remember him glaring at me with so much hate, I thought he was going to charge over and hit me. I can't blame him for wanting to. Gabriella's lies have no boundaries. He doesn't know because she isn't telling him everything. Instead, he said, "If you so much as breathe a word of this to *anyone*, I'll have you thrown out on the streets to fend for yourself. You hear me?"

He didn't give me time to answer before he stormed out of the room. Sometime later, I heard angry yells from their bedroom and Gabriella's dramatic crying and pleading.

I kept the note. It's scrunched in my hand still, the ink staining my skin red. The only reminder I have that it was real. That it really happened.

Breathing out with frustration, Dr. Fraud shifts in her seat, knowing I won't talk. She then prescribes me medication that won't work.

Nothing will. Because my nightmares are real. Just like the monsters are.

CHAPTER THREE

My room in Stonehill is bare. A single metal-framed bed with gray sheets and a brown throw is shoved against the wall. A tiny television and blank journal sit on a cheap wooden desk with a matching chair. The only window I have is small and has no curtains. None of them do after a girl used them to hang herself a few months back.

My muscles are tense and have been since last night. He got into Lawrence's home. Got past security without being seen or heard. Surely this place would be a walk in the park for him?

I *know* he'll find a way to get in. To get to me.

Pulling my knees to my chest, I uncrumple the note he left for me, reading the words a few more times to torture myself some more. I don't know why I do. It's not as if the letters are going to change.

He found out about the baby, somehow. A mistake must have been made.

Gabriella had Lawrence take care of it. It isn't in any record, and the hospital staff who dealt with me were paid off. But this is Blake Santos. He's always made it his business to know everything about me.

A harsh knock on the door snaps me from my thoughts. I'm used to the noises here—the screams, shouting, and banging of minds losing sanity. But I'm not used to someone *knocking*. That's a privilege girls at Stonehill don't have, and I immediately think of Blake's games, knowing he would do something like this for effect.

Knock, knock, Heidi, baby. Let me in.

Doing this in broad daylight is new. Careless. Then again, haven't I always conjured something insane in him?

I wait for a nurse to barge in, but the door remains shut, the person on the other side waiting for an invitation. Shooting a quick glance at the clock, I realize the nurses are doing their rounds and don't usually arrive at this section until half an hour—

Bang, bang, bang.

My frown deepens. This isn't Blake's style. He at least lets the threat linger for more than a few days before unleashing fury. But if it isn't him, who is it?

Slipping off my bed, I take a step, seeing the shadow of someone looming beneath the door. My heart pounds against my chest as I reach out and grab the handle, knowing Blake would be too impatient to wait like this.

I pull the door open slowly, and when I see who it is, my body freezes. *Fuck.*

MILTON: WORSHIP

A man stands in the place Blake should be. A man I believed to be dead and someone I thought I'd never see again. I shake my head, bewildered, in disbelief.

"You-You're dead."

As a smile tilts his lips, I realize how... *different* he looks. He isn't the same as I remember, not at all, and for a moment, I think maybe I've made a mistake. But, then, there's no way I would ever forget a face like his—the face of the man I had killed.

Swallowing is hard. My underarms and palms dampen with moisture as he stares down at me. When I was fifteen years old, the very night Blake stole everything from me, a man named Milton walked through the door and put a bullet into a man's head who tried to attack me. To this day, I don't know why, but he'd made a brutal impression, and Blake made him my reluctant bodyguard.

But this Milton isn't the same as I remember.

Dark brown hair is now short at the sides and longer on top— handsomely styled instead of messy. Not like the times it was damp from the rain after he rode his motorcycle through the murky streets of Fair Haven doing Blake's dirtiest deeds. Even the stubble on his chin and upper lip have been tamed. Shaped. He's wearing a suit, one tailored to his tall, lean frame. Not the thick leather jacket that brandished Horn Hill MC's slogan, *Devil Horns*.

No, he never looked like *this* before. Polished and clean. Even the way he carries himself is miles apart from the man he was when he was a club member. And I know I'm in trouble because if this is the same person, he's probably seeking revenge.

"Heidi Adams?" I jerk back, unnerved. He's *British*? There was always a twang of something I could never make out, but it wasn't an accent, and certainly not someone from England.

My heart thumps in my chest fast, my stomach queasy with shock. "W-What? You *know* that's my name?"

He ignores me. "I'm Milton Xavier Hood. Nice to meet you."

Meet me?

He's holding something in his hand. A brown folder Dr. Rogue had. *My* folder. Coldness slithers down my spine, not understanding what the fuck is going on. Is this a trick? A game?

"Now that we have that out of the way, may I?" Barging past me, he walks inside my room. My heart swells with discomfort when he shuts the door behind him. I move back. It's too small in here to put space between us. Yet, he only observes the place, eventually making his way over to my bed, where he picks up the note I left on the sheet. He reads the words and says nothing, dropping it back down.

Watching him move around the room is both unsettling and fascinating. That this is the same Milton I knew less than a year ago. Pulling out the chair, he takes a seat, as if this were some normal situation. Folding one leg over the other, he rests the folder on his lap, eyeing me with a meticulously trained stare.

I don't know what to say or do. Run or stay. Both seem like they would have the same outcome. Both sound foolish.

The name he called himself comes to mind then. It was always *just* Milton. Milton Xavier Hood sounds like an entirely different person altogether. Someone important. *Feared.*

And I do fear him. I always have.

Milton moved up the club's ranks quicker than any Prospect ever had, as he often did everything Blake wanted efficiently. *Cleanly.* He became one of the best, better than Blake's own son, Nicolas. I should've known Blake would keep him alive. After all, why kill someone that useful?

"Your file was quite the read. Very…interesting." Flicking open the folder, his thumb brushes over the mugshot of me secured to the page with a paperclip.

Am I hallucinating that he's here? Has being trapped within the walls of Stonehill for only a few months affected me so soon? "What are you doing?"

His eyes watch as I move further back until my back bumps into the wall, furthest away from him. "Excuse me?"

"Why are you pretending you don't know me?" I run my hand over my face. "I-I mean, you're really here?"

He slaps the folder closed and turns to the journal on the desk. Reaching over, he scans through the pages, the corners of his mouth lifting when he sees it's empty as if he knew they would be. "Dr. Rogue, unfortunately, had to take emergency leave, and I've taken over during her absence."

"Stop."

"Stop what, Miss Adams?"

"Calling me that!" I shout, shuddering from the boom of my own voice. "You're dead. I saw you leave with Nicolas. He had blood on his clothes. *Your* blood."

"Well, as you can see, I'm very much here, aren't I?" He stands then. "Tomorrow, we will have a proper meeting. Six o'clock, evening time."

I glare at him heatedly, something inside of me snapping. "Screw you. I don't know how you're here, but you're not taking me back to Blake. Not this time."

"Be ready at eight." With one last prolonged stare, he moves past me and walks out, leaving the door wide open for the fall chill to come inside from the hallway and wrap around my body. My mind reels. Oh, how the tables turn, and keep on turning.

Who knew it was the dead I should have been looking out for. Not the living.

GABRIELLA'S FACE CRUMBLES WITH DISGUST AS SHE TAKES A TINY, reluctant sip from a white foam cup. It's filled with cheap, *soul-black* coffee. And she forgets she used to be as cheap—probably why she pulled the face.

She loathes it here. Detests sitting at the greasy, plastic tables on the uncomfortable chairs. Nothing but judgment plasters her face whenever there's a scream from a recovering addict begging for a hit like she's never once screamed for it. *Probably* still does.

I'm not sure why she's here and wish she would go away. Milton was here yesterday when he's supposed to be dead. I need to try and pull together some semblance of understanding as to how that's possible. When I saw him last, he was being led away by Nick on Blake's orders. Forced to take the long, condemned road to the Hill. As anyone who goes up there never comes back down.

Having not slept, I'm too tired to deal with Gabriella, assuming she needs to discuss something that requires orderlies at the ready and a table separating us. Not that I care what she is about to break to me now. Her flair for the dramatics is irritating, given the more important things going on.

"Poor Ashley had to go home. Her father has taken ill." Putting the cup down, she flips open her purse and ruffles inside. Pulling out a compact mirror and a tube of lipstick, she takes the lid off and smears it over her lips. An expensive shade of *bitch*. "It's such a shame. I thought she was finally making progress with you." After she's done, she finally makes eye contact with me. "Lawrence thinks you shouldn't come to the wedding."

Finally. The actual reason why she's come.

I'm not surprised. I expected it after Lawrence's reaction at the house. Still, that doesn't stop the pang of misery that spreads through my chest and stabs me deep inside. It's closely followed by a wave of hatred at myself for caring. For *feeling*. "Oh."

She plays with her necklace—a nervous habit. Or not. I know she's enjoying this deep down in her dead heart. "Yes, and not to the house anymore either. At least, not for a while." Her left eye unmistakably twitches, revealing the lie. *She* doesn't want me there, probably because Lawrence is one step away from learning her secrets. "It's too stressful and putting an awful strain on our marriage. Not that you care." Sniffling, despite her eyes being dry, she leans forward. "*Nothing* was there when I checked the surveillance. No one broke into the house. You say it was Blake, but he doesn't know about the baby. It's *impossible*."

I shift restlessly at the mention of his name out loud. "It was him."

"It *wasn't*," she snaps. "Lawrence believes you brought the coffin into the house yourself after Elise announced her engagement, and I'm inclined to agree."

"When do you suppose I had time to do that? And wouldn't the driver remember if I asked him to take a detour to the graveyard so I could dig up my dead baby? God forbid you to believe the truth for once."

"Do not talk to me like—" Her body flinches as I abruptly stand, like she's expecting me to reach out and smack her. I bet she wants me to. Mark her face, so she has something to show off in front of the cameras. I walk away instead, knowing she doesn't deserve the energy. "Where are you going?"

"Away from you."

"Don't walk away from me!" she yells angrily. "Heidi!"

CHAPTER FOUR
FOUR YEARS AGO

Trailing my finger lightly over the ink engraved along my sister's skin, I admire the sizable black skull hauntingly shaded in the middle of her spine. Red roses surround a ghostly face—disturbing and beautiful and *very* permanent.

"Did it hurt?" I ask, amazed she got a tattoo despite Mom banning her when she asked if she could get one a few weeks ago.

Only whores get tattoos, she had said. *No way!*

"Like a bitch," Nicole grunts, leaning upon her elbows to take a pull from the cigarette between her fingers. My nose wrinkles, hating the smell. "For a freebie, it's not bad, is it?"

Some guy from her group of friends gave her a tattoo. Being seventeen and needing parental permission, he offered one for free, under the condition that he could tattoo whatever he wanted on her skin as a piece for his portfolio. She jumped at the opportunity and was gone all last night, sneaking back in during the early hours this morning while I was pretending to be asleep. "Why did you get it there?"

"Why do you think?" she scoffs. "You know Gabriella would have a seizure if she found out I got a tattoo. Put this on for me, would you?"

Sitting up on my knees, I grab the tube of cream from her hand. After gently massaging a generous amount into her skin, I cover it with gauze and secure it with tape. "Okay, done."

Jumping up from the bed, she drops the cigarette butt into an empty can of coke and throws her shirt back on, winking when she catches me watching. "You wouldn't even know it's there."

"I'll give it a week." I smile playfully, knowing she will get clumsy with hiding it and inevitably start another war with Mom.

I pick up my small mirror and gaze at my reflection, wondering what I'd look like with a tattoo and if I'd suit it—something little like a bird or a flower. Sighing deeply, I place the mirror down. I'm not edgy like Nicole is. There's no way I'd ever pull it off.

"Heidi?" She's by the mirror now, staring at me in the reflection as she fluffs her dyed black hair. "I'm going to a party tonight."

"Okay, I'll cover for you."

"Actually…I'm taking you with me tonight." My eyebrows rise with surprise.

It's no secret Nicole lives on the wild side as she has since she turned sixteen. It usually includes parties, dancing all night, and drinking with boys.

Falling through the door drunk every weekend has caused friction between her and Mom, getting worse the older Nicole becomes and when she chooses the wrong paths.

She's more secretive about her partying lifestyle now, only because I help her to be, covering for her when she needs to spread her wings and fly—as she calls it. As Mom and Dad's fights worsened, becoming abusive toward each other, Nicole's been the only one to hold me while I sobbed. Lying to my parents is worth it when it makes my super outgoing sister happy.

She's never asked me to go to a party with her before, and I don't understand why she is now. I've never been to one. Not even drank. I went to a sleepover at my best friend, Georgie's, house a few weeks back. We ate pizza and binge-watched *Gossip Girl*. A far cry from the stories Nicole tells me about the parties with her friends.

"Well? What do you think?"

I shift uncomfortably. "Why?"

"Why not?"

"You've never asked me to go before?"

"Well, I'm asking you now. I want you to meet my friends," she says excitedly. "It's weird that you are constantly in here reading books all the time."

"I hang out with Georgie."

She laughs. "You are aware she won't be your bestie forever, right? Once she goes off to her fancy college, you won't hear from her ever again. It's a fact of life."

My shoulders sag, the thought saddening me. Georgie and I are inseparable, friends who wear matching bracelets that signify forever. I can't bear the thought of us never being best friends. "I don't have anything to wear," I sigh, a spark of annoyance shooting through my chest at her persistence.

"And you know you have no say in this, right?"

"Mom will find out, and she'll argue with Dad again."

She waves her hand dismissively. "They sleep in separate beds, Heidi. You going to a party won't change shit that's already broken. If you love me, you'll say yes."

I grit my teeth, and she grins because she knows she's gotten her way. "I hate it when you do that."

"Say it, or I'll think you won't love me," she demands stubbornly, and I know she won't back off until I agree.

"Fine...I'll go."

"That's the spirit!" As she goes over to her wardrobe, I flop back on my bed and gaze up at our cracked ceiling, not knowing why she wants me to go so much. I know her friends are older. They won't want to be around a high schooler. I'll embarrass myself, and Nicole will end up hating me, getting frustrated by my *childishness*. "Aha! What do you think?"

My eyes bulge at the skimpy black number she's pulled out of her wardrobe. A scrap of material that leaves nothing to the imagination. It's thin, short, and has rips in inappropriate places, on *purpose*. She laughs at my reaction.

"I'm taking that as a no?" I scowl, and she shrugs, eyeing the dress with appreciation. "Your loss, I'll wear it." Tossing it on her bed, she goes back to looking. Then she gasps. "This!"

I warily look at the next dress she's chosen. Although it's slightly better than the black one, it's still not something I'd ever dream of wearing. It's a dark red camisole dress with spaghetti straps and made from some sort of satin material. "It's...*short*."

"Your point?" She throws the dress at me and then a pair of black heels, causing a tightness to form in the pit of my stomach. I don't see why I can't wear my jeans and a T-shirt.

"I don't—"

"I'm taking a nap before we get ready," she interjects, yawning widely and ignoring my despair as she throws herself down on her bed. She falls asleep in minutes, soft snores filling the silence. And all I do is sit there, fear chilling my bones.

Because I don't want to go, and I have no idea how to get out of it.

NICOLE RAPS ON A METAL DOOR THREE TIMES. A PEEPHOLE screeches across the center, and a pair of bloodshot eyes peer out, narrowing into slits when they land on us. The shutter closes, and the door opens with a guttural moan. "Get in."

After stepping inside, the door slams behind us. The man who let us inside is tall and bald, yet has the bushiest beard that hides his mouth and neck. He's terrifying, parts of his face covered in splotches of black ink—symbols of some sort. "You're late," he says through clenched, crooked teeth.

Nicole rolls her eyes. "I'm here now, aren't I?"

Suspicion crosses over his eyes when they come to me. "Who's the bitch?"

"My sister." The weight of her arm falls against my shoulder, and I can't help noticing how cold she feels. Still, I cling to her, wary of the man in front of us and the way he's ogling me. "Doesn't she look like me, Deuce?"

"Nah," this Deuce guy taunts. "She looks *better*." My body recoils as he laughs huskily, sounding like Dad after smoking too many cigarettes. "You better get goin'. You don't want to keep him waitin.'"

"Yeah, yeah." Slipping her hand into mine, the back of my throat aches with dryness as she pulls me down a dark corridor.

"Nicole?" I tug on her hand, but I'm not sure she can hear me over the music blaring from beyond.

Having not felt warm all night, my teeth chatter, even since before Nicole woke up from her nap earlier. While she showered, I tried to think of a way I could get out of going. By the time she came back and started getting ready, chatting animatedly, and telling me it would be the best time of my life, I'd lost my nerve, not wanting to upset her.

She helped me get ready, putting makeup on my face and taming my blond curls. I looked pretty, which was strange for me to see, as I'd never dressed up or put makeup on before. I resemble Mom when she goes out on the town, which I often admire about her.

"What underwear are you wearing?" Nicole asked after putting on the dress she chose for me. It only came to mid-thigh, and I felt bare as I showed her the white cotton panties with a bow on the front that I was wearing. She slammed her palm against her forehead. "God's sake. Take them off."

Going over to her drawer, she pulled out a black thong and dropped it on my lap. "Um...I-I don't—"

"Put it on, Heidi," she snapped impatiently, and my bottom lip trembled, emotion bubbling inside of me. Sighing, she said softer, "Just put it on, okay?"

Not wanting her to be mad at me, I put it on, even though it was so uncomfortable. When it was nearing ten at night, we left, walking through the backstreets of Horn Hill, to a place I least expected to end up.

Parked out front of a dark building sat rows of motorcycles, even though it seemed lifeless outside. When Nicole said a party, I thought of a house full of teenagers her age. Not *this*.

The choking fumes of smoke and liquor parade under my nose as she pushes a door open. Keeping hold of my hand, we enter a large room where harsh music assaults my ears. It's loud and obnoxious, and I want more than anything to cover my ears with my hands to block it out.

The place is teeming with men, all different shapes and sizes. Sitting around tables drinking and dressed in the same leather apparel as the man who answered the door, eyes hungrily follow the few women in this place supplying them the liquor they demand.

As fear fills every crevice inside my body, I squeeze Nicole's hand in an attempt to get her attention again. She ignores me and continues guiding me through the smoke-hazed gathering. As we pass one table, a man suddenly whistles loudly. There's a sharp sound of a slap, and Nicole winces. "Damn, girl, I'd love to be all over that." That's when I realize he smacked her ass.

Plastering a fake smile on her face, Nicole turns to him. "I'm taken."

"Wouldn't stop me." He chuckles, his eyes following her as she continues taking me down a narrower corridor until we finally come to a door at the end.

"Heidi?" She hesitates before knocking. "Promise me something?"

"What?"

"Do everything he says. Please. For me?"

Before I can ask what she means, the door opens, and a guy not much older than her stands in the doorway. The gray in his eyes deepens to charcoal, sending a wave of unease down my spine.

He, too, wears black leather like the rest of the men from the other room. With ashy blond hair, I have a feeling his attractive face is all but a lie, hiding whatever truly resides inside. "Where have you been?" he demands, tone gruff and irritated.

Straightening her back defensively at his words, it's like something unspoken passes between them. Something that isn't nice. "I had to sneak out, but I don't answer to *you*."

Pushing past him despite the dangerous haze in his eyes, she drags me inside a different room. Sickness swirls in my stomach as I take in the medium-sized space, a long, wooden table dominating the center. Or perhaps it's the four men seated around it, seemingly in the middle of a conversation.

Clouds of thick smoke float overhead as my attention comes to the man at the head of the table. The first word my mind can conjure up is that he's *enormous*. Unlike the rest of the men here, donning the same leather jackets with a slogan on the back, he's wearing a shirt with the sleeves rolled up, a few buttons undone at the neck. Tattoo's cover his thick muscular arms as he listens to one of the men speaking, occasionally lifting his hand to suck the end of a cigar. Silver runs through his blond hair, the same color as the ash falling onto the table.

Eventually, his stone-cold eyes swing our way, as if he were purposefully drawing out noticing our arrival. "You're late."

"I-I'm sorry," Nicole says meekly, something he doesn't seem impressed with. When he stands, I crush her hand, a grin spreading over his lips as he moves around the table—something I least expect from such a brutal-looking person. Everyone else has gone quiet now, all eyes on us.

"You look like someone who doesn't have what they owe." His voice is deep and menacing, the closer he gets to us.

Nicole shakes her head. "No."

"That's not good enough."

"I...I know," she replies, her voice shaking. She's scared of this man, and for a good reason, as he looks like someone straight from a nightmare. "But I do have something else that might interest you... a-as payment."

Tilting his head to the side, he holds her stare for a moment before his gaze finally settles on me. And I want more than anything for the ground to swallow me. He laughs. "You shouldn't have."

He goes to turn away, but Nicole steps forward bravely. "Please, Blake. It's all I have."

Peering back, he eyes me again and sighs with frustration. A hand then slips into my free one, and a gasp flies out of my mouth. "Come with me," the guy who answered the door says, offering a strained smile I think to try and relax me, only it far from works. "I'll get you a drink."

"N-No—" Nicole's nails dig into my hand. I cry out as she glares at me. *Do as he says.* "Nicole?"

The moment she lets go of my hand, he pulls me away. She doesn't look at me as he takes me into another room adjoining this one, slamming the door closed behind us and blocking my view of her.

Panic flows through me as I frantically peer around the room. It's big and spacious—a bedroom with a king-sized bed covered in dark purple sheets. Nothing much else. A few bits of furniture. A table with a lamp. A worn rug—

"Come over here," the guy says, an undercurrent of pity in his tone. Or is it boredom? Bringing me over to the bed, he sits me down, and my legs quake as he kneels in front of me.

"What's going on?" I question. "What does she owe?"

Not saying anything, he instead lifts his hand and flicks a curl from my face. After a second, his hand drops, and he swears under his breath. "Do you know why you're here?"

"Nicole said it was a party."

"You know it's not, right?" My heart sinks so deep I might be sick. I know this isn't a party now and that Nicole's in some sort of trouble. "What's your name?"

"Heidi," I answer. "I don't want trouble. Can I please go home?"

"Not tonight." He stands. "Stay here while I get you that drink… You're going to fucking need it."

Turning, he walks out of the room, leaving me on the bed. Tears burn my eyes as his words echo inside my head.

Not tonight.

CHAPTER FIVE
FOUR YEARS AGO

As soon as he's gone, I'm off the bed and running for the door. "No," I gasp when it doesn't open. I'm locked inside. Why has he locked me inside?

Pressing my ear against the wood, desperate to hear Nicole's voice and hoping she hasn't left me here, the sounds are incoherent, but I do catch the words *money* and *snow*.

I can't tell if Nicole is still there or not. Maybe they wanted me out of the way so they could talk privately, and this is a stop before we go to the real party. Surely when she said friends, she didn't mean these people. Maybe—

My thoughts trail off, something bitter and cold wrapping around my throat. Curling my arms around my body, I know deep down Nicole meant to bring me here. I wish I knew why.

Footsteps behind the door pull me from my thoughts. Stumbling back as the lock clicks, the guy comes back inside, lips pulled tautly, and eyes obscured with something I can't name.

Shoving his hair out of his face, he pushes a glass filled with something dark at me. "Drink it. All of it."

"What is it?" My hand trembles so severely, some of the liquid sloshes over the rim. He glares at me, and it's enough to send a shot of fear through my stomach. Bringing the glass to my nose, I cough when strong fumes burn my nostrils, the smell of it awful.

"If you know what's good for you, you'll drink it." There's a warning in his words, and I'm afraid to say no. That he'll hurt me if I don't do as he says.

Lifting the glass to my lips, I take a sip. Rolling his eyes with impatience, he puts his hand on the bottom of the glass and forcibly tilts it back until I have no choice but to drink all of it or let it spill down my front. The taste makes me gag and lights a fire down to my stomach. While I fight the urge to vomit, he takes the glass from me and pushes me back to sit on the bed.

"Where's Nicole?" I hiccup. "Will we be able to go after she's finished talking?"

He sighs. "I told you, you're not going anywhere tonight, and neither is Nicole."

"Why?"

"Enough with the fucking questions." He plonks down in a chair opposite the bed, searing me with a burning scowl from across the room. My bottom lip wobbles as we sit in silence until I hear something that turns my blood to ice.

Nicole screams.

Jumping up from the bed, my hands fly to my mouth with terror when a slap rings sharp, followed by a crash that sounds like chairs toppling over. "Sit down," the guy orders, but I don't listen. I can't.

Shuffling back, I don't stop until my back hits the wall furthest from the door, as if being away from it will make me feel better. When there's another scream, my knees give, and I sag to the floor. Tears flow out of my eyes, my chest heaving up and down.

What's happening?

If I thought this night couldn't get any worse, the door opens, and Blake walks inside slowly, one hand in his pocket and the other holding a cigar. Lifting it, he sucks on the thick end, blowing out heavy, gray smoke as he closes the door behind him.

"Why is she on the floor?" he asks, his eyes on me. The guy shrugs, and Blake steps forward. "Stand up."

Using the wall as support, I get up, afraid of what will happen if I don't. Both men stare in a way that makes my stomach twist, but it's Blake's stare I feel the most fear from, especially as he rakes down my body like he's trying to find something about me that he might like. When his lips curl upward, bile threatens to spew past my lips, reminding me of those times boys at school would leer and shout out at me, calling me all kinds of nasty things.

When he takes another step forward, my back presses into the wall—something that seems only to amuse him. "Do you think she's worth the money that cunt sister of hers owes?"

The guy, who is now leaning forward, breathes out audibly. "I don't know, Pops." Are they father and son? "She's young. It might be more hassle than it's worth."

"Hmm," Blake murmurs thoughtfully, facing me again. "She's a pretty thing, alright. The rest of these bitches in here are getting loose and dirty. I'm up for a challenge. A little kitty to train."

"You'll have a hard time keeping the rest of them off her," he warns. "Look at her. A couple more years and she'll be the best-looking bitch in this place."

Blake's lips slither into a smile, and something about it is cruel. They're speaking about me as if I'm not in the room. Almost as if he's doing it on purpose, Blake takes another few terrifying steps forward and laughs when I whimper. Like this is a game, and I'm entertainment. It's not long before he's in front of me. So close. He's on my skin even though he isn't touching me. Staring down at me, smoke and spicy aftershave bind around my neck. It's in the back of my throat, bitter and tangy.

My muscles stiffen when he pulls his hand out of his pocket and lifts it to my face, raking a calloused thumb over my cheek. "I'm going to have fun with you, baby." Grabbing my hand, he tugs me forward. "Come. I want to see you."

"Please," I whisper as he takes me back over to the bed. Sitting, Blake positions me so that I'm standing between his long legs.

"Can I leave?" the guy asks.

"No. Stay," he says, not taking his eyes off me. Off my face. My hair. My body. "You think I don't notice, Nick?"

"Notice what?"

"That you don't *fuck*." He turns to face him. "I admit—we need a good clear out. Get some new bitches in. But even on our rides, you don't fuck the whores. The guys have noticed. *I* have noticed." Nick shrugs, but it's clear Blake is making him uncomfortable. "If you want to be a leader one day, you have to be a man. Those pricks out there will eat you alive when I'm gone. They won't follow a pussy who won't even fuck a pussy. You got that?"

He nods, though it's evident he's angry given the way his nostrils flare. "Yeah, Pops."

"See this as your first lesson. Sit and watch how a *real man* does it." Letting go of my hand, Blake leans back on the bed. I want to move, run, but I'm rooted to the spot. "Take off your dress, babe."

My eyes bulge, hands instinctively flying up to grab the straps of my dress. I can't take off my dress. Nicole told me not to wear a bra. She said the lining of it would show through, and it would be stupid. All I have on is that thong she made me wear.

Made you wear.

More tears blur my vision and stream down my face. "Put music on," Blake says, waiting for me to obey his command I don't want to follow. Standing, Nick goes over to the stereo I didn't notice in the corner of the room. After pressing a button, the guitar shrieks through the speakers loudly. "Come on, baby girl. Take off your dress."

"W-Why?"

"Because I said so," he says, his tone darkening. Coldness impales me when he mouths, "*Off.*"

My head shakes, but the action causes the room to spin. Before I know what's happening, I feel myself falling forward into Blake, who catches me. "Fucking hell, *Nicolas*. How much did you give her?"

"Not a lot," he defends, though I sense he's lying. "She won't pass out."

Grunting, Blake stands, and a gasp flies out of my mouth when my feet suddenly leave the ground. Carrying me over to the bed in his arms, he places me down on top of it. My body sinks into the middle of the mattress as he sits next to me, and I want to move away, but my arms and legs are heavy and weak. I can't move. *What's wrong with me?*

I let out a cry. Despite being unable to move, I'm hyperaware of everything, like Blake's hand running up my thigh. He lifts my dress slowly, bunching it at my hips, and blows out a heavy breath when he sees the underwear I'm wearing.

"Damn, baby girl. I think that deserves a round of applause." He claps his hands together and laughs. "And maybe a reward. What do you think, son?" Nick says nothing, and Blake's eyes narrow. When he waves his hand for him to come over, my heart drops. "Come here, dickhead."

There's a shuffle, and then Nick appears next to me, shadows beneath tired eyes. "What?"

Blake claps him on the back, hard enough to make him wince. "I'm only doing this to teach you. You're afraid of pussy."

"I'm not—"

"Stop lying," he growls. "You're not strong. You're not ready to be a leader of this club. Not *yet*. Now, let's get you reacquainted with the cleanest, freshest pussy in this place, all ready for you to *eat*."

His eyes widen. "No, Pops. She's yours—"

"And she will be, but I'm too pissed off to reward her, and I just want to sink into a nice, tight, *wet* hole. She's too fucking dry."

I open my mouth to scream, but can't. That's when I spot the empty glass Nick gave me on the table. It was him—the reason I can't move. He drugged me.

Shifting to the side, Nick takes Blake's place and doesn't look me in the eye when his fingers catch the thin material of my panties. "Don't be so fucking gentle. Snap it."

Furrowing his brow, he tugs until it breaks. It's viciously ripped from my body as Blake then reaches out and tears my dress right down the front as if it's nothing more than tissue. I can't believe this is happening as Nicolas lifts my legs around his shoulders and leans in closer.

Cold air nips at me as tears endlessly trickle down the sides of my face. I try to scream again but can't. Even as his hot breath blows against my inner thigh, lips brushing against my skin.

My breath is sharp as I inhale when his tongue flicks out and licks me. The sensation is strange and twists my stomach into knots. I don't like it as he sucks and licks, followed by an uncomfortable pinch as one of his fingers slips inside of me. I whine in pain as he pumps them in and out, fingernails scraping the inner parts of my flesh. My eyes squeeze shut.

Stop. Stop. Stop.

He doesn't.

"Good girl," Blake whispers, sitting on my other side. Reaching over, he touches my breast, stroking my nipple. My lower stomach clenches as something unbearable claws through my body. They both keep going until I no longer feel like a person. Just a thing they're both poking and prodding in ways they shouldn't.

After a while, Blake taps Nicolas' shoulder.

"Enough." Nick stops and gets off me, expression pained for a few seconds before disappearing, and Blake chuckles. "There you go. That wasn't so bad, was it? Now get the fuck out."

Turning away, Nick gets up and leaves the room, slamming the door behind him. Blake's mouth stretches wide. "Now it's my turn."

Lips slam against my mouth, his tongue thrusting past my teeth. It's more like a brutal assault than a kiss, and I gag at the choking invasion. Reaching down to his pants, he undoes his belt. "Your sister handed your soul over to me, baby girl, and now you're all mine," he says, popping the button of his jeans and tugging them down.

Put it on, Heidi.

Do as he says.

My world fades. Nicole planned this?

The more my thoughts try to piece together what's happening, the more I can't help thinking that she had no intention of taking me to a party tonight. She offered me over to Blake to save herself from whatever trouble she's gotten herself in, and the realization of that shatters my heart. I can't believe it. Why would she do this to me?

I cry silently, trapped in a drug haze.

Even though I never asked, Nicole often explained what men's penises looked like, but I don't expect Blake's to look like this as he pulls his boxers down. It's horrifyingly big and thick, a bulging vein throbbing angrily down the middle. It's hard, poking upward, and the thought that he's going to put it inside of me breaks me.

Sliding his hand down my stomach, he touches my body roughly, groping and mauling parts of me that no one has ever felt. Then he grabs himself and breathes a laugh of surprise.

"I've not been this hard in a long time." He breathes out, face wrinkling with pleasure as he strokes his erection. Catching me looking, he grins. "You like?" My teeth grind together when he unexpectedly forces a finger deep inside of me, now tender from when his son did it. "So tight. You're going to hurt me."

Taking his finger out and smearing wetness over me, he forces my legs wider apart and rubs the tip of himself against me. Then, without warning, he's pushing inside and splitting me open.

Pain.

It's cutting. Intrusive. *Wrong.*

I can't breathe or think of anything but this agony.

As he pushes inside me again, my head smacks off the headboard hard, and everything goes black. My head throbs, as if my skull has been split open. "I haven't come from a pussy in a long time. Not since Nick's mama," I hear him say but can't see him, head dizzy and stomach nauseous.

But I still feel his attack, every bit of it.

What a strange sensation it is to feel yourself slipping away, only to be yanked back as scorching vomit spews past my lips. I'm choking on it, and all he does is laugh. "Oh, no, you don't, bitch."

Bending me over, I vomit on the floor at the side of my bed. Once I finish emptying the contents of my stomach, Blake's flipping me back down, and then I'm gone again. Maybe Nicolas did overdose me. Maybe I did hit my head so hard I'm dying. It makes it slightly easier to pretend this isn't happening. It will all be over soon. He will go away, and then I can go home.

"Wake up!" He slaps me across the face. My eyes open just as he's tugging on the end of his blood-soaked cock. Grabbing me around the throat, he drags me closer as hot semen shoots from the tip and lands all over my face. Yelling out in pleasure, he drowns me in his acid, body convulsing, and shaking.

"That's right, baby, take it." Lifting his hand, he rubs it into my face and hair. "You damn beautiful bitch."

He collapses on top of me, spent breaths blowing against my neck. There I lie, a monster on top of me, heart ripped open and a virgin no more. And finally, I die. At least, that's what I pray to happen.

CHAPTER SIX

My door bursts open, and I wake with a start as an older nurse named Vera enters my room. "It's time for your meeting."

Sitting up, I rub my eyes, noticing it's dark outside now, and I slept most of the day after Gabriella's visit. Six o'clock only means one thing—Milton and my impending doom. I can't seem to swallow the lump in my throat as I stand.

I was hoping I'd imagined him as I follow Vera out of my room and down the hall. When we get to the far end of the corridor, we stop beside a set of double doors that I've never been down before. "Keep going until you reach the end."

She doesn't make a move to follow as I pass to the other side. As I glance back at her, I notice she's not *looking* at me. Tired eyes avoid mine, and I think it's on purpose.

I begin making my way down the corridor. Soft, classical music plays in the background, building up to a crescendo the closer I approach the white doors at the end. It's an exquisite piano piece that threatens to soothe my nerves. Drop my guard.

I'd be an idiot to let it.

Finally, I enter a large room with a high ceiling and tall windows when passing through the other doors. It doesn't feel like I'm in the same building anymore. It's spacious in here, with black wooden floors and antique suede couches—nothing like the old, rickety furniture in the patients' wing. The clinical smell that frequents the hallways has now been replaced with the scents of jasmine and musk.

It's familiar and all Milton, transporting me to when I was on the back of his bike with my arms clinging to his waist—

Heels tapping on the floor snap my attention to a woman approaching me. Dressed in all black, her hair pushed back into a chiffon knot, the only thing bold about her appearance is the blood-red lipstick that coats her lips—something her thin bone structure doesn't really suit.

"Good evening, Miss Adams," she greets me in a British accent, like Milton's, which only confuses me more. "If you want to take a seat, Mr. Hood will be with you shortly."

She then exits the room before I have a chance to say anything, leaving me no choice but to sit and wait.

As the minutes tick by, my insides coil tighter. It's not long before footsteps echo around me. Like the footsteps outside my bedroom door in the club. Those times he used to sit outside my room whenever Blake was on the road, protecting me from any other fucker who wanted what their leader had.

Heavy. Assured.

Twisting my head to glance over my shoulder, the Milton I don't know finally rounds the corner wearing another suit—this one gray with a black waistcoat. I hate the way my body reacts. How I can hardly catch my breath as he makes his way over to me, finally reaching me.

Shivers tumble down my spine, and I can't look at him in the eye, not even as he says, "Follow me."

Taking a deep breath, I reluctantly get up and follow him. We go into another room—a private office with the same color scheme as outside. Fire burns logs in the fireplace; the flames angry and bright, casting an orange glow against the walls. "Take a seat." I eye the only seat I can take opposite his desk.

My heart jumps to my throat when the door closes behind me. Milton moves around me. He unbuttons his jacket and takes a seat behind the desk once he's in view. As his body leans back in his chair, moody eyes watch me like never before. Not when he was in the club. Not even yesterday when he came to my room.

"I insist you sit unless you want me to force you. It's up to you." Knowing he'd do just that, I move over to the chair and sit on the edge. A few moments of silence pass until finally, he says, "I was just finishing reading through your recent report." He opens my file that's on the desk in front of him and shuffles through the papers. "Shall I read it to you?"

"I don't care."

Standing with the folder in hand, he moves around the table slowly. "Heidi refuses to talk about what happened." Eyes pin me with a curious stare. "And what is it that happened?"

"This is getting boring, Milton," I say with clenched teeth. It's in my file. Why is he making me say it?

"Tell me."

I squeeze the leather seat with my fingers. "I took tablets for a headache."

"How many?"

My nails puncture through, hating that he's doing this. "Until the pain went away. Do you want an exact number?"

Hiding his smile, his gaze drops back to the file. "Heidi deflects from issues that are discussed, tending to blame everyone but herself. Attention limited. Little to no regard for anyone else's feelings and is considerably detached from her own. Lies continuously about bad things that have happened to her." He pauses, glancing at me over the pages. "Now, that's something I can agree with."

My heart almost fails right then, and I'm rendered speechless. *He knows what you did to him.* But he doesn't know why he—

"She has no ambitions, dreams, or goals outside of the facility. Refuses to participate in the activities provided. Long bouts of depression. Bad social skills and a lurid sense of the world around her—"

He slaps the file closed, and just as I think he's about to address what's in it, he turns his back to me and throws the entire thing into the fire.

The pages catch and burn, and I swallow hard. "Is that supposed to make me feel something?"

"Does it?" Turning back to face me, his eyes lower to my body, something that makes me uncomfortable because I know what I must look like—a terrible mess.

"How are you here?" I whisper, emotion welling in my throat.

Moving forward, he's stops right in front of me. "Stand up."

"What will you do if I don't?" I challenge, and there it is, the slightest flash of something in his eyes that look so fucking black in the firelight, showing me just a hint of the person I knew.

His chest rises and falls in a silent sigh. "Something you won't like."

"Go ahead. You don't scare me," I snarl. "Nothing you do will be any different to what I've already been through."

Grabbing my arm, he roughly pulls me off the chair and out of the office. Pushing open a different door, we're suddenly outside and in a private parking lot. He marches me in the direction of a sleek black car. Rain spits at me, and my body shivers from the cold.

"No!" I dig my heels into the ground and pull against him. It only makes him tighten his grip. "You're not taking me back. I'll fucking kill myself before you do!"

He slams me up against the side of the car, hard enough to make my spine cry in protest. Water seeps through my clothes and chills my skin. "I'm *taking* you to dinner."

"Do you think I'm buying that?"

"Actually, I am." I shiver when his eyes rake down my body once again. It's not sexual. He doesn't desire me. If anything, he looks disgusted, which bothers me more than I like. "If you don't get in the car, I *will* put you in myself, and we really don't want that now, do we?"

Not wanting him to touch me, I open the door and get in. Once I've settled over the leather seat, he backs up and slams my door in my face. My teeth chatter as he gets in next to me, and while my instincts scream to run, my legs are like lead and won't move, knowing what this man is capable of.

He fires up the engine, but before pulling away, he locks gazes with me. Since I arrived at Stonehill, people haven't looked at me in the eye. It wasn't long until I realized it was because they don't *want* to see me.

Milton sees me, staring at me with eyes I once couldn't get out of my head. *Still can't.* He thinks he has me all figured out, but I'll have to show him that he doesn't. "Are you going to behave?" he asks.

"Fuck *you.*"

"I'll take that as a yes." He turns on the heat and then the radio, backing out of the parking space. After leaving the lot and driving down a private lane, I realize he doesn't go into the city. He takes old roads instead, avoiding the main ones. Sticking to the shadows like he knows nothing else.

Eventually, we pull up outside a small building in a secluded area with only a few townhouses. The engine dies, and he gets out of the car first, circling around the back and opening the door for me. Once I'm out, his hand falls on my shoulder, probably to stop me from running from him.

Keeping me close, we approach a black building with red accents and dimly lit inside. A place that looks too romantic for the likes of Milton and me. The aroma of food instantly makes my stomach growl as we enter, reminding me that I haven't eaten all day. Only a few are in the restaurant, and while it should relax me that we're in public, I know not to be. "Milton?" A tall woman approaches us with a wide smile. Wearing a fitted black dress and killer heels, her hair is a deep shade of ebony that makes her tanned skin glow. As I look closer, it surprises me to see the eyes of a predator peering back. Ones that barely hide a salacious and deviant appetite.

"Bella," Milton says as she leans over and places a kiss on his cheek. One that's not too lingering or makes contact.

"It's been a while." I shrink under her assessment when she turns to me. "*Bellissimo.*" She smiles. "*Lei è tua?*" A muscle works

Milton's jaw, and her eyebrow rises when he doesn't answer. "Very well. Your business is your own."

Unexpectedly, she reaches forward and takes one of my blond curls in her fingers. Her eyes soften, tongue dampening her lips.

Fingers snake around my waist and Milton pulls me back against his body, breaking her contact. The heat from his body flares through mine as he says, "A *table* Bella, please. I don't have all night."

Her back straightens defensively, reminding me of a feral cat. "Of course. Right this way."

We follow her to a table, and I scoff when Milton pulls out a chair for me, as if this is a date or something. "How are the kids?" he asks Bella then.

"Up to no good." She places menus in front of us, and he flicks through his. "Would you believe my Rika turned twenty just yesterday? And she's still available if you're looking to settle down, Milton."

He smiles at that. "You must be desperate to get her out of the house if you're offering her to me."

She laughs and asks, "Drinks?"

"Water will do." Nodding, she walks away, and he watches her leave for a few seconds as if he's thinking about something. "Order whatever you like," he eventually says to me.

I don't grab my menu. A ring on his middle finger has caught my attention instead. Something I've never seen him wear before—a silver signet with an 'X' engraved on the metal. Something that looks significant. Important. Catching me looking, he twists it with his thumb. "Do you want to know what it means?"

I know it's a trick question. This means something to the new Milton, and he *wants* me to ask the question he knows is burning the tip of my tongue.

Shame that I'm also a firm believer in what you don't know can't kill you.

"A story for later maybe," he says as a girl walks over to our table carrying our drinks, Bella now nowhere to be seen. She's pretty, with golden skin and silky black hair, only she looks out of place, playing a waitress in a restaurant lurking on the edges of the city.

Curving the ring around his finger again, Milton watches as she places our drinks on the table and pulls out a notepad from her pocket. "Can I take your orders?"

"The tagliatelle."

She points her gaze at me, and I immediately glance away, avoiding the mirror that reflects my own fear and pain. She doesn't hide her feelings well. No one taught her how. "Same," I mumble in reply.

After writing down our orders, she leaves, disappearing through a door that I assume leads to the kitchen. Minutes pass, and the silence continues. I sense Milton watching me again, and I shift uneasily, tugging my sleeves over my arms, self-conscious of the scars from my previous attempts to end it all.

"Still hiding them, I see." His expression is void of emotion, but his eyes are once again so dark. I want to tear my gaze from his, but I can't. I'm sucked in. How can he be the same person I knew all those years ago?

"Finally, waking up from a seizure, I see."

"And still *irritating*." He lifts the glass of water to his lips and gulps down half of it.

"Why did you burn my file?"

He shrugs. "Did you want to keep it?"

"Let me guess—you threw it into the fire to wipe any trace of my existence because you're trying to make me disappear?" I jump when he slams the glass down on the table, and for the first time tonight, there's real annoyance in his expression.

"Is that not what you wanted to achieve the night you shoved pills down your throat?" There's an edge to his tone now. "To disappear?"

My shoulders tense. "At least that was on *my* terms. Nicolas clearly didn't kill you, for whatever reason, and now you're here to take me back to Blake, as you always do. Am I right?"

The side of his lip curls upward. "Couldn't be more wrong."

I grip the sides of the chair until pain shoots up my fingers. "Why are we having dinner?"

"Because you look like a corpse." He drains the rest of the water while I flush with shame. *A corpse*. How nice of him. "At least you looked alive last time I saw you."

"I couldn't have been more dead."

He opens his mouth to say something but closes it when two figures approach us. Men wearing heavy jackets, rumpled jeans, and boots now stand by our table, an unmistakable air of danger surrounding them. With eyes void of humanity. Not the worst I've seen, but something I recognize well.

"*Quanto?*" The taller man steps forward, reaching into his pocket and producing a thick pile of cash.

Milton's calmness is unsettling, and all he does is sigh. "It seems I still can't bring you anywhere without attracting attention. Do you know what he just asked?"

I don't understand the word, but the cash in the man's hand and the way he's leering at me with sweat trimming his brow, makes it obvious. Too many people have looked at me like that over the years. Too many have wanted to possess me. *Own* me. "They want to buy me."

As I wait for Milton's next move, it dawns on me that maybe he isn't on Blake's orders after all. Perhaps this is his plan—get revenge on me for having Blake order his death by selling me off.

"Take it, fucker. We pay you good money." The man throws the cash on the floor, and the bills splatter over the tiles. So much. I should tell him damaged goods aren't worth that amount.

My heart speeds up as I brace myself for history to repeat itself. Instead, Milton surprises me by *laughing*.

His laugh punctures the strained atmosphere, causing people in the restaurant to glance in our direction. Like mine, their faces twist with confusion at the disruption.

It stops, and Milton's out of his chair in a flash. A glint of metal shines in the light as he grabs the man's shoulder and thrusts the knife he's holding into his neck. There's a sickening squelch as he yanks it back out and stabs again, this time twisting the blade.

"She isn't for sale, *fucker*," he sneers as the man splutters on his own blood that drips down Milton's hand. "*You* take it."

Blood roars behind my ears as the other man shuffles back, eyes wide with horror as Milton drags the knife back out. Blood sprays on the floor, the money, like raindrops. After yelling something incoherent, the man runs out of the restaurant as his friend's body drops to the floor. Dead.

No one screams.

A few people get up and leave, but those who remain go back to their meals like nothing happened. It's so fucking silent except for my heart that's thumping like a drum. I breathe in. Out. I'm not sure I'm even *breathing* at all.

Sitting back down at our table, Milton tosses the bloodied knife to the ground. Grabbing a napkin, he wipes the blood off his hand as Bella rounds the corner, skidding to a stop when she sees the man's body sprawled out on her floor.

"You should know that it's rude doing business in public, Bella," he says to her, his tone stern. Angry.

Her hands ball into fists, eyes lighting with rage, and I realize then this was orchestrated by her, not him. "Things are changing around here, Milton. Perhaps it's time to pick a side."

"I have a side, thank you."

"If you could even call *that* a side—"

"How about you say that to Maxim? I'm sure he'd love to hear it."

Just as Bella storms away, our food arrives, and I can't believe it considering there's a dead man on the floor a few feet away from our table.

As Milton wraps pasta around his fork, unaffected by murdering a man, he glances at my untouched dish. "Eat. It's going to be a long night."

I want to scream at him. Run. But years with Blake have destroyed normal human emotion, and I don't know what to do other than pick up my fork and copy his actions. Chew and swallow.

The line is thin between knowing better and craziness. And I'm leaning more toward crazy. To survive, you have to be.

Dark gray clouds drift in front of the moon, encasing everything in darkness as we drive further away from Fair Haven. My bones rattle after what happened in the restaurant, yet it confuses me.

Blake killed. He murdered people who wronged him. Who so much as looked at him the wrong way. He killed men, women, and often in front of me. So why has Milton murdering that man shaken me like this? Because he killed to *save* me without Blake telling him to?

No, I don't trust him. I *can't*.

I don't know where he's taking me. He isn't bringing me to Blake's or back to Stonehill. He drives the opposite way, over Fairdell Bridge and out of Fair Haven.

Soon, we leave the highway, veering on to a much smaller road with sharp turns and bends. The wheels kick up spray and throw dirty water over the windshield. The wipers come on automatically, clearing away the water, revealing an isolated, bumpy road thick with foliage and woodland trees.

The bit of food I managed to shove down my throat turns in my stomach. Being someplace secluded with Milton sets my nerves on edge. He's a cold-hearted killer, so maybe selling me off was too dull.

As I imagine him dragging me out of the car by my hair and killing me too, I'm left even more mystified as the road smooths and trees thin. That's when I see it; a three-story mansion made of black stone sits spectacularly lit on an incline. I've never laid eyes on a place like it, and wariness pulsates through my body because the unknown is a damn scary thing.

We meander up a circular driveway and stop outside. The large front door, trimmed in gold with two stone columns positioned on either side, opens, and a man smartly dressed rushes outside as Milton gets out of the car.

As I fumble with my belt, transfixed on my surroundings, he opens my door and waves me out. My legs wobble as I exit the car. This isn't a home, it's too formal, and I'm aware that my Stonehill attire doesn't go with a place like this. God only knows why he's brought me here.

"When I'm leaving, bring the SUV around," I overhear him say to the valet, tossing the keys at him. It starts to rain again as the man gets into the car and drives it away.

My shoulders sag, knowing tonight is only getting started. The real reason for me being here only minutes away from being revealed. I'm exhausted and miss my bed in Stonehill, yearning to be under the covers and pretending I don't live in a world like this. With buildings lurking in dark places in the middle of nowhere.

"What is this place?" My spine stiffens when his hand lands on the small of my back, his heat radiating through the material of my shirt. He leans in, and I inhale sharply at his closeness, not wanting it but gravitating toward the warmth. He's always been warm.

"You'll see." Tingles spread through my body as his breath brushes against my neck. I know I should resist as he guides me toward the door. It's almost as if the mansion itself has cast some imaginary power over me, stunning me into compliance.

Or maybe I'm just too far gone now, and I've all but accepted my inevitable fate.

As we step over the threshold, I tilt my head to the side, soaking in the strangeness of the foyer. With silver granite floors and harsh gray walls, the hallway is cold and masked in shadow. It's a place I don't want to be, but also can't help the curiosity, especially noticing the three archways perfectly aligned with three directions to take.

Right, left, or forward.

All lead to darkness. Unknown places of secrets I sense they hide. The only decor in the room is the three colossal silver Xs displayed directly across the entrance, like the ring on Milton's finger.

The tightness in my chest is unbearable now, especially when male laughter and music hints that we're not alone.

"This way." Milton's arm wraps around my waist as we go left through the arch, down a straight corridor. Moonlight spills through huge windows, casting a glow against his frame, like some twisted version of a halo.

Since leaving the restaurant, his face has been formidable, secretive of his true feelings. But for the first time tonight, the harshness has softened, and it's like he's relaxed being here.

Or it could be just another lie his face paints. I can't tell anymore.

Finally, we reach a set of thick solid doors with golden handles. Letting go of me, he digs into his pocket and produces a black card with another X on it. Swiping it through a scanner, there's a *beep*, and the doors unlock.

As soon as he pushes me inside, my mouth drops open. The room we've just entered has high ceilings and onyx marble floors that shine. The walls and furniture are decorated in deep brown, burgundy, and gold. It's big, spacious, and fancy, like something straight out of an old movie.

"Gentlemen," Milton greets a group of men gathered around the bar wearing tuxedos. They all nod in a polite reply as we pass them, but their eyes don't linger for more than a few seconds. Almost as if it would be impolite to do so. *Or foolish.*

The chatter continues behind us as he takes me down a quieter corridor, stopping outside another door. When these open, all I see is red. My eyes strain against the harsh ruby glare. Lights that reflect off the white walls, the contrast, unlike anything I've ever encountered.

As my eyes adjust, I peer apprehensively at stairs that lead down. I know better than to ask questions, but they sit heavily on my tongue. Any minute they're going to slip down my throat and strangle me.

The door automatically slams shut behind me, and I can't take it any longer. As Milton goes to grab me again, I step away from him. "No." Sweat dampens the back of my neck, knowing there's danger waiting for me down there. What else would there be? "What the hell do you want from me?"

"Now that..." He takes a step closer, and my back hits the door. I wait for him to touch me. Hurt me. It doesn't happen. The fucker does nothing. "Is the best question you've asked me all night. And all will be revealed if you shut up and keep moving."

Grabbing my hand, he forcibly pulls me down the stairs. I try not to trip over my feet as panic grips me. Once we reach the bottom, I don't like the look of the long, windowless hallway ahead. Something that seems completely endless.

Appearing devilish in the red light with splatters of blood on the front of his shirt, Milton's hand wraps around my waist again. Taking me deeper into what my brain can't stop calling a modern-day Hell.

Every so often, we pass a black door but don't go into any of them. Unease churns my stomach. He's dragging this out too long. I even expect Blake to open one of those doors, arms wide open and signature evil smile in place.

Let's go home, Heidi, baby.

But the doors remain shut, and we keep walking. As my thoughts pick away at everything that's happened so far , nothing has made sense. This isn't for Blake. Milton's doing this for himself, and I think that terrifies me more.

CHAPTER SEVEN
FOUR YEARS AGO

There's an unbearable pulse behind my eyes as they peel open. The pain cuts through my skull as I try to focus. The room is blurry, but I know where I am. I'm still *here*, in a place girls like me aren't supposed to be.

I'm not at home in bed, wearing my fluffy warm pajamas. I'm naked, exposed, my skin ice-cold from a draft coming in from somewhere. And I remember everything. Every sordid, terrible thing that he inflicted on me.

I almost want to pretend that I don't remember. How nice would it be to pretend none of this happened? That Nicole hadn't brought me to this place, and I never laid eyes on these people. Especially *him*. That horrible, terrible monster.

Something's on me—a tickling sensation I imagine it a spider on the hunt for a meal, though knowing it can't be anything other than a trick my mind has made up. Because whatever's touching me is what woke me in the first place.

Blinking away the sheet of fog, I tilt my head to the side, and there he is. Blake. Damp hair and clean clothes indicate he's fresh from a shower. Black shirt that's tight against his thick chest and jeans. He smells of soap and aftershave and has a crazed grin on his mouth.

My head splits open, and everything he did to me comes flooding back in. The most prominent was the expression on his face when he raped me. Tears burn behind my eyelids and eventually seep down my face.

"Hey there, sleepyhead," he says, sick smile in place. I try to move as he circles around me, but my body spasms when sharp pain slices through my stomach, gushes of blood pooling between my legs, stinging broken skin.

"Ow," I groan, sobbing.

He sits down next to me and touches my arm, turning me to face him. I squeeze my eyes shut, not able to look at him. "Baby girl. You're making me feel bad." He chuckles, and I know it's not guilt he's feeling. "Come on. What we did together was special." Disgusting lips press against the side of my face, and my entire body recoils. He doesn't like that reaction. "*Look* at me."

A threat underlines his tone. Not wanting to be hurt again, I reluctantly open my eyes to see his smile widening, but there's nothing nice about it. It's sick and twisted, just like him. I've never hated anyone as much as I hate this man right now and what he did to me. Grabbing me, the tips of his fingers indented in my cheeks, he kisses me on the lips, tongue thrusting deep into my mouth. Whining with disgust, my hands slam into his shoulders to push him off. He's too firm, and for a few more agonizing seconds, I'm trapped against his mouth until he finally stops.

"I've been telling the boys what a ride you are." He strokes my head, pushing sticky hair off my face. But then his fingers wrap around the strands at the back of my skull, and I cry out from the bite as he pulls my head back. "You surprised me, baby girl. Making a man come like that is dangerous. It...*complicates* things."

Bending over to collect something from the floor, he holds it up to display a pink housecoat with a tie. "You like? I took it off one of the girls. Put it on. I don't want any old cunt looking at what's mine."

"Please," I dare whisper. "Can I go home?"

"Home?" He chuckles. "But this *is* your home."

"It's n-not. My mom—she'll be looking for me and Nicole."

He throws the housecoat at me, and it hits me in the face. As if the mention of anyone looking for me has hit a nerve. "*No one* will be looking for you. I own you now. And if you *ever* try to leave me, everyone you know will die. Now. Put. It. On."

Sobbing, I slip my arms through the fleecy sleeves, ignoring the blood and bruises. I just want to be covered. After securing the belt into a tight knot, he grabs my arm and pulls me off the bed. As my feet hit the floor, I let out a sharp, pained breath. Not that he cares as he proceeds to drag me toward the door.

My teeth clamp together as I try my best to concentrate on walking through the agony. Blake takes me out of the bedroom and back into the room with the long table. It's empty now, no soul in sight. How long was I passed out?

His arm then falls over my shoulder, and he kisses me on the side of my head as if we're *together*. The weight of him almost has my knees buckling as he takes me back into the room with all the tables and men.

There are less than before, and the women are still here. I find my sister easily. Sporting a black eye and cut lip, she stares at me under Blake, eyes vacant. Hurt stings my heart. I can't look at her, unable to face her betrayal.

"Blake." A thin and small man approaches us. Greasy hair plasters his forehead, his tongue running over his lips as he eyes me. "You finished with her yet?"

Terror catches me. Any moment, I expect Blake to push me at the man. *Share* me. Instead, his arm around me stiffens as a cold smile stretches over his lips. "No."

"Come on." The man steps forward, and I notice we've caught the attention of most of the room now. I spot Nicolas leaning against the wall furthest away, arms folded and watching. "Why do you get the young pussy and not your boys?"

Blake pushes me behind him. "Listen up!" His voice booms out, addressing the room. "I know most of your dicks are hanging off because of the dirty pussy in here." I catch the women exchange terrified glances. "I'll get you all new pussy, but this bitch right here is *mine*. Anyone touch her, and you will be sent to the Hill—"

A scream tears past my lips as a hand grabs the back of my neck. The surface of the table hits my face, and I'm stunned with the agony.

As hands grab mounds of the housecoat, trying to tear it from my body, a loud bang suddenly cuts through the room. A weight falls against my back, something hot and wet dripping down my neck and onto the table. Blood.

"Bullseye!" Blake laughs crazily, pulling the skinny man off of me. I let out a terrified scream as I look down and see that his eyes are still open, desire dying out. I fall to the ground, kicking my feet to put space between myself and the dead man.

"Milton," Blake says, eyes fixed at the entrance.

Standing by the door and dressed in all black with a gun in hand, stands a man I believe might be the devil himself. Dark, cold eyes connect with mine before going back to Blake. "Hope he wasn't a friend."

"Been trying to find a reason to kill that fucker for months," Blake chuckles, and I can't believe he's laughing when there's a dead man on his floor. "You still looking for a job?"

"Yeah," Milton replies. "What you got?"

I'm dragged to my feet, a hand grabbing the back of my neck. Blake's lips slams against mine. It's a brutal force, and my lips feel bruised after he's finished. Then, he tosses me at the man—Milton. Arms catch me and hold me there. "Kill anyone who touches her. The bitch is *mine*."

CHAPTER EIGHT

I'm starting to believe this place is nothing but a maze of closed doors that hide mysteries I'm better off not knowing.

As Milton continues leading me through this place, I've been trying to keep track of the tunnels we venture down, and how many turns we take.

Though, easier said than done, given that every damn one appears the same. Nothing stands out that might set them apart, and I think it's on purpose, to confuse those unfamiliar with the layout. It's a harrowing reminder that there's no way I will find a way out if Milton gives me any reason to run.

After passing another row of black doors, we finally stop outside one like the rest. After unlocking it, he lingers behind me, a silent order for me to enter first.

Ambling inside, my lips instantly part as I take in the room we've just entered. The red glare is gone. Standard lighting shows we're now in a large space painted black. Leather couches sit opposite a long open fire embedded into the wall. However, the flames are the only thing warm about this place. There's not much else in here—a sleek black table and ceiling-high shelves with books and other inanimate objects. Nothing to Gabriella's taste; she would complain about the masculinity and gothic design. "Would you like a drink?" Milton asks, his presence still behind me.

"Just get on with it." The quiver in my voice makes me cringe, betraying my nerves. How much longer can I keep this up?

"Patience." Brushing past me, he crosses the room and goes through a different entry. When I hear what sounds like a cupboard bang, I whirl around and grab the handle, twisting and pulling. As I knew it would be, it's locked, but it was worth a try—

"Going somewhere?" I spin around. He's back, holding a glass of red wine. His tie is missing, the top button of his shirt undone, and hair slightly mussed as if he's just run a hand through it. Shaking his head, he moves over to the couch and takes a seat. "How do you suppose to get outside and find your way back to Fair Haven in the dark? Granted, you manage to get past security...and my dogs."

"You're keeping me prisoner?"

He takes a sip from the glass and smiles behind the rim. After swallowing, he lowers it to the table. "I haven't made up my mind. Sit."

My insides shudder with unease. He could be messing with me further, and knowing emotion drives his decisions, a knot forms in my stomach. He hates me, and hate leads people to do heartless things. Still, I know I'm going to have to play along if I want him to reveal what the hell he wants from me.

I sit away from him on the opposite couch and cross my arms over my chest. "Why am I here?" I know time is only a commodity to men like Milton, yielding it however they want. Whatever way suits their victim.

"Because I want you to be."

"Stop." My fists clench on my lap. "Delaying the inevitable for whatever desired effect you're trying to achieve isn't going to work."

"You're right, I am delaying. But maybe I like seeing how much I get under your skin."

Anger claws at my insides. "You haven't gotten anywhere, and your efforts of pretending not to know me were hilarious given I know who the fuck you are. How could I forget *you*?"

He leans back, hair falling over his face. He doesn't move it away, and it only makes him ten times more intimidating. "And that's when I tell you you've never known me. Not in the slightest."

"What do you want?"

"What do you *think* I want?" he counters.

"I thought revenge but taking me here…now I think you want something else. Surely a man who brings a girl into a basement of a mansion desires something fucked up, wouldn't you think?"

What I say rolls off my tongue, admittedly too well, and he laughs. "Your defense mechanism is tacky, and now I know why I found you in Stonehill."

"Right," I call his bluff. "All those times at the club, you didn't once wonder why Blake was so obsessed? Why he had you put bullets in people's heads for me?"

"You tell me?" He's amused, and it unsettles me. Shifting again, he leans forward, this time resting his elbows on his knees. My heart stops, the action reminding me so much of the man who watched me walk across the room, waiting to strike down anyone who so much as tried to touch me. "Don't get shy on me now. Go ahead."

My lips press together, and he breathes a laugh as if knowing there's no fight left in me. Instead, I ask the obvious, "What is this place? Why am I here?"

"A private club. Of sorts. And as for why you're here...well, I don't know whether to put a bullet in *your* head for what you did or something else. Something...*fucked up.*"

"Does what I did matter seeing as you're still living and breathing?" He bristles, the tension flowing between us about ready to explode.

"And now you're just pissing me off." He gets out of his chair, and my back presses into the couch instinctively. "You don't want to deal with me when I'm angry."

Even with him on the other side of the table, I stand to try and put more distance between us. But his long legs make it easy for him to circle around and close in on me. Slamming his hand into my shoulder, he pushes me back down. "I didn't say get up."

I slam my fists into the couch. "Just get this over with and shoot me then! You think I don't know how this goes? I wronged you, so kill me. We both know you're good at that."

"And give you the easy way out?" Leaning over me, his hand pressing into the leather by my head, his finger traces my neck. I breathe out slowly, my heart racing. His touch tickles my skin, and my nails dig into the couch. He's never touched me like this before, and just as I'm about to question if I like it or not, his hand drops. "No. You owe me too much to put you out of your damn misery."

"I owe you *nothing.*"

"We'll see about that." The smell of him surrounds me. Intoxicates me. The darkness in his eyes revealing its game over. "You'd be dead if it weren't for me, or have you forgotten how many times you were on death's door, and it was me who stopped you from falling through the threshold? Blake wasn't going to save you. Not Nicolas. Not *even* your own sister. You would be nothing but an addict letting any dirty cock down her throat for a hit."

"You're disgusting," I sneer.

"And your idiocy cost me from getting what I wanted. The whole reason I was in that dump in the first place."

Confusion wriggles my brow. "What are you talking about?"

He laughs, but it's cold. "Do you think I was there to follow that fucker? To bow down to *him*?"

Blood pounds in my ears, and I don't understand. He was so devoted to Blake. To the club. Is he really telling me that was a lie?

"You messed things up, and now you owe me. All for telling Blake it was me who slid between your thighs." Hands slap down on my legs, and I yelp when he grabs them. "Nicolas couldn't *wait* to tell me how it was you who stabbed me in the back when he had a gun on me. Who knew the little damsel in distress had it in her?"

He squeezes, and I grab his wrist, digging my nails into his skin. Not that it fazes him or lessens his brutal grip. "It wasn't—"

"Wasn't what?"

"It wasn't like that! It's true. I did lie, and I regretted it the moment it left my mouth."

"Not only that..." Bitterness drips from his voice now. Disgust. "You put me down for *him*. I didn't get what I needed to get because I fucked the Devil Horn's *princess* to save the *prince*."

"No," I whisper, sickness balling in my stomach, reminding me of all the terrible things that've happened.

"Denying it?" When I don't reply, he catches a handful of my shirt and pulls me off the couch. *"Answer* me."

My stomach flips upside down, and fear takes over as he glares down at me. "Please, Milton. He was going to—"

"Don't *beg*," he rumbles. "Begging will get you nowhere with me."

"What are you going to do?"

"Always the victim. Don't you get tired of listening to yourself?"

It angers me when hot tears splash down my face. My arms pathetically flail in an attempt to push him away, but his grip on my shirt only tightens.

I give up. "Do you think I care what you're going to do?"

"You *should*." Letting go, he grabs my wrist and tugs me over to a different door. I pull against him, not knowing what to think as he shoves me inside a small room with just enough space for a double bed. There are no blankets or pillows, only a mattress covered with a black sheet.

Black candles light up the room, and as shadows flicker across the stone walls, everything inside of me screams that it's time to run.

"Sit," he orders, flinging me toward the bed. I cry out, my stomach colliding with the mattress. He's never been so rough with me, and my insides hurt at his malice. He stands at the mouth of the door, thunder in his eyes, like when he killed that man at the restaurant. "Revenge sounds too sudden. You fucked me over, so it would only be fair to fuck with you."

"You know how bad Nick was getting. He was going to kill Nicole if I told the truth. That he was—"

"Unbelievable." He shakes his head. "You saved a sister who not only locked you in a cage but threw away the key herself. You can't get any more *pathetic* than that."

"I know *you* wouldn't understand. I bet you haven't a single person you care about in your life. You only saw a half of what Blake and Nick did to me. You have no idea all I've been through."

"I know, alright."

"No, you don't. You're a man," I spit venomously. "Nothing *ever* destroys a man."

"Oh, but men can be destroyed," he says, jaw hardening. "Then again, I expected as much given we both know how self-centered you are. A poor, fucking princess."

"I'm...I'm not." I glance down at my lap, losing the defiance. The fight. *Just get it over with.*

Stepping forward, he grabs my chin and forces me to look at him. I avoid eye contact, not wanting to see his anger toward me anymore. "You care too much about the people who don't give a shit about you."

This time, my eyes flicker up to his, and my belly stupidly flutters at his fingers beneath my chin. But they die when he grabs my wrist and pushes me back onto the bed.

Climbing over me, he picks up something I can't see until he's wrapping it around my wrist. That's when my eyes bulge at the leather cuff he's strapping me down with. One that's attached to the bed with a thick metal chain.

"What the fuck are you doing?!" I reach over to fight him, but he grabs me quickly and closes another cuff around my other wrist, trapping me in. "Milton. Take them off!" I pull against them, but it only hurts, and it seems like the heat in the room has intensified. "I can't... I can't breathe."

"That's better," he says, getting off me just before I can kick him in his groin.

"Let me out. I'm going to..." I'm going to faint. The coldness of unconsciousness threatens to drag me under, settling on the back of my tongue.

"But seeing you like this pleases me. Given I almost had what I was looking for until you ruined it, years' worth of work destroyed, and now you'll pay for it."

He stops by a table, and leaning over, blows out multiple candles at once. My heart explodes in a frenzy of harsh beats as he blows out more candles. Then another. Two more. He's doing it slowly, dramatically, because he knows I hate the dark. The bastard *knows*.

"Milton, please... You know how it was in there. I didn't think they'd send you to the Hill."

"Bullshit." He puts out another candle, and I pull against the restraints, twisting my wrists, yelping with pain when they cut me.

Another flame dies, smoky wax filling the air around me, smothering me. I choke on my tears as he blows out two more candles. With each candle he distinguishes, the room darkens, the shadows creeping in. Tears pour down the sides of my face, despair seeping in like poison. "It's true. How can I prove that to you?"

"It doesn't matter. I don't feel like letting you out." Another candle goes out, and he's down to the last few. "It's not just what you did. The problem that lies between you and me is a different entity altogether, and you fucking know it."

My bottom lip shakes. "Don't leave me in the dark."

"Give me a good reason why I shouldn't?" He lingers by the last few lit candles that shroud half his face in shadow.

"You know I hate the dark."

"I know." He blows out the last candles, and I'm plunged into absolute darkness.

"Milton!" I scream as the door opens brief enough for me to see him leave. He doesn't look back as he walks out of the room, slamming the door behind him.

Leaving me alone in the darkness I hate.

Hours tick by. I don't know how many to be sure, but I know I've been here for a long time. As Milton walked away, I screamed and yelled and begged him to let me out.

He didn't come back, not even when I cried harder, screamed louder, and pulled against the cuffs so hard, the tapered sides of the leather sliced into my wrists.

I gave up, and without meaning to, drifted off. Then the nightmares crept in and threatened to send me into hysterics. I woke up screaming. Pleading all over again. And even then, there was no reply.

"Why am I here?" I ask myself that one question I never seem to get an answer to. Why am I still *living* if this is all it's going to be for me?

When I was at the club, I hated the dark. I could never see where Blake was. Could never anticipate or prepare myself for whatever he decided to inflict on me next. And it was always in the dark that he would carry out his most heinous acts.

"You're fucking insane," I say out loud, using my last bit of energy to say what I'm about to next. "I'm glad I told Blake it was you. That I lied. Do you want to know why? Because I fucking *hate* you. You need to go to Hell where you belong!"

The door opens, and a breath of surprise whooshes out of my lungs. Squinting at the bright light that shines inside, Milton's dark form stands in the doorway. "I don't think the devil and I would get along."

"I find that hard to believe."

He smirks. "And you have no idea how close I am to dragging you down to it with me."

"Go ahead." He goes to grab the door, and I gasp. "Wa—wait! Don't close the door. You've made your point. I'm the worst person in the world. Don't you think I know that already? Bad choices I make always come back and haunt me. And I suffer. Believe me, I suffer. Isn't that enough for you? Wait… am I…"

"Bleeding?" Breathing out heavily through his nose, he leans his shoulder against the frame of the door. I'm only realizing now that my wrists *hurt*. "Yes. Those cuffs you have on cut if you struggle. Which you've already demonstrated. My design. For if you take blood from me, I shall from you."

He's right. My hands and down my arms are soaked with blood, staining the fabric beneath me. Dizzily, I look away, closing my eyes. "I always wondered what it would feel like to bleed out."

The bed dips, and Milton uncuffs one of my wrists. I feel him inspecting the cut now pumping blood, enough to make me feel funny. Light. *Cold*. "You probably won't last the night with these wounds."

I try to laugh, but it comes out strangled, and I pull my arm away. "Why waste your time with me, Milton. I bet there are better things you could be doing."

My eyes flicker in his direction. He's staring down at me, and I don't know when it happened, but something's changed with him. What, I don't know.

When I attempt to sit up, the room whirls. Damn, I really have fucked up my wrists. How did I manage that?

"You should find someone who would be more fun to torture," I go on. What am I talking about again? "Like Florence. Do you remember her?" Florence was one of the new girls Blake got for his men. An eighteen-year-old prostitute, so stunningly beautiful, it hurt to look at her. "She liked you. I'd bet she'd even let you fuck her."

She used to annoy me by continually going on about Milton and how much she wanted him. Though, it seemed he was never interested in fucking her. And *everyone* was interested in fucking her.

"She's dead." As he stands and moves away, it sinks in what he said. Florence is dead. We had our differences at times, but weirdly, she was family.

"Did—did you?"

"Not my doing." His tone is hard. "She didn't do anything to me. You, on the other hand…"

"That's too bad that she's dead, and you're stuck with me," I whisper, hoping he will leave. And I'll bleed out. And it'll be heaven. "Because I will never let you fuck me."

Lying back down, I rub my palm over my face, so tired. Weak. He says something else, but I don't hear. My brain shuts down, and my eyes close. I give up. And all I can do is pray I don't wake up.

CHAPTER NINE

It could be morning or night when I wake.

It's hard to deal with the weight of exhaustion inside, the pain in my head pressing down on the backs of my eyes. For a moment, I think I'm still in that room. I twist my wrist just a little to see if any pain follows. There's no sting. Nothing strapping me down. Who knows, maybe I imagined it all?

No Milton. No torture. No *feelings*.

As I open my eyes, the first thing I see is light coming from an expensive crystal lamp on a dressing table on the other side of the room. Stonehill doesn't have such nice things. And I'm lying in a different bed, one that is much comfier than my own. Super soft pillows and a heavy comforter keeping me warm and sleepy.

I'm alive. Fuck.

The bedroom is beautiful; expensive dark furniture and blue-gray walls. I try to think about how I ended up here until remnants of what happened come back to me in flashes.

Milton. Torture. Feelings.

A door bangs in the distance, and my heart jumps to my throat. Even though there's no way I can know it's Milton, I sense that it is. Somehow.

And just like that, he walks inside the room before I'm ready to face him again, stopping when he sees I'm awake. Every muscle in my body seizes, and that's when I notice my wrists wrapped in bandages. Like one of the suicide girls from Stonehill. "What time is it?" I ask, my throat scratchy and sore from all the screaming I'd done. Screaming, *he* made me do. He takes a seat on the bed next to me, and I lean away.

"It's nine in the morning. You've been out for hours." He glances away, eyes void of anything. "A car will arrive for you shortly."

"A car?"

"Yes. To return you to Stonehill."

"What's that supposed to mean?" He watches me for a moment before eventually standing. Wearing another fancy suit—this one navy—the man from last night is gone. He's stone. "It means we're done here."

An acidy laugh escapes me, the pain inside my chest confusing me. Tossing me away like trash after only just reappearing back in my life should make me happy, yet I'm far from it.

"What's changed?" I'm not sure what sick part of me wants to question him. He wants to take me back. *Great.* But I don't get it. "You were so hellbent on making me pay, and now it seems you can't wait to get rid of me?" My voice blisters with emotion. Too much. I can't control it.

"Careful. Anyone would think you *enjoyed* what I did to you." I push the blankets off me and drag my body out of bed. Cold air nips at my skin. My pants and Stonehill shirt are gone, and all I have on is a discolored bra and my Stonehill panties.

My cheeks flame. "You undressed me?"

"Nothing I haven't seen before," his voice is cold. Detached. "They were covered in blood."

"Because of *you*. Letting me go just means you tortured me for no reason. I knew you wouldn't have the balls to see it through—"

"You think that was torture?" His eyebrow rises. What the hell is wrong with him?

My fists clench, and I snarl, "Fuck *you*, Milton. I think I'll go with my first assumption that you were looking for something to get off to—"

"Is that so?" He steps forward, and my legs scuffle back, but he keeps coming at me until the backs of my knees hit the bed. I suck in a breath when he leans over me, his fists pressing into the mattress by my legs.

"You're right," he says. "Handcuffing girls to my bed *so* gets me off." It feels like my heart stops beating as he crawls up the bed until his body is hulking over mine. "I mean, look at you. Such an *attractive* sight." My hands tremble as I cover my eyes, the heat from him, the smell of him, unbearable. Nice. Hot.

He grabs my hip with his large hand, and I squeal from the contact. "Stop." He eyes me darkly, irises smoldering.

"Continue begging. Your consent doesn't turn me on," he growls through gritted teeth, every word dripping with venom.

"Milton, stop, you…you—" Peeking through my fingers, he's glaring down at me, resentment etched into handsome features.

"Say it." My head shakes, and I sob when he captures my hip and pins me against the bed. "*Now*."

"Monster."

Something crackles between us. I feel it as his grip tightens on me. "You're right. I am. And I suppose I should show you how monstrous I can be." I lose my breath when he grabs my thighs and forces them apart.

"No!"

"I think the only way to make you pay is to punish you like this..." Keeping me pinned down, he presses himself against me. And that's when I feel his hard erection straining his pants, grinding against my core. "Stay fucking still. If you move, I will put you back in that room."

Keeping me against the bed, he moves down until his face is between my legs. My breaths come out quick and ragged, my insides clenching with unease.

I cry out when his fingers stroke me over the material of my panties, the sensation jolting through my entire body. I hold my breath when he does it again, and again, each time, shoots of disgusting pleasure ripping through me.

When his finger hooks the side of my panties and moves it aside, I try to buck him off. "Don't—"

He grabs me and forces me still. "I don't think monsters take no for an answer, Heidi."

"You can't." Saliva dries on my tongue when he licks me. "Ahh!" I'm not expecting it, and my body bucks as his tongue glides over my clit. I can't catch my breath as he takes me completely into his mouth and sucks.

My eyes roll back. What. The. *Fuck*.

Slapping my hand over my mouth, I bite down on my fingers, needing to stop this. We shouldn't be doing this. This was never meant to happen between us. A burn of something brews in the pit of my stomach as he continues licking me out, and I can hardly believe that I'm getting off to him doing this to me.

That my body *likes* it.

"Milton, please," I groan as he continues the onslaught, never letting up. Not stopping for a pause. I moan louder, the sensation he's causing building into something that shouldn't be building. And just as I'm about to come, just as he's about to force what I think is my first orgasm out of me, he stops.

The loss is painful as he removes his mouth. I almost scream, but the look on his face stops me. Wiping his lips against my inner thigh, he smiles cruelly, and I know why.

I stay down as he gets off me, between my legs throbbing mercilessly and tears pricking my eyes. "Now you have a reason to call me a monster. And look at that, *you* were the one getting off on it."

Storming out of the room, he slams the door shut behind him. I stay still. Very, very still, knowing I almost came for a man I hate. And for someone who hates me.

CHAPTER TEN
TWO YEARS AGO

Blake's solid body presses into my back. With one hand restraining my head against the wall and the other holding my hip, I can't move, can't escape his attack as his pelvis drives me into the wall. Grunting behind me, the smoke from the cigar dangling from his lips suffocates me.

As he often does, he's playing one of his many games with me. This one—though not the worse I've been through—is *endurance*. How much can I take before I crack? A game only he wins. And as I often do, I go as far away as I possibly can. I think about anything. Everything. *Nothing*. Even when he catches a mound of my hair and drags my head back, bracing his hand against the wall to show me his fingers streaked with blood—*my* blood. I look away, not sure how I'm still alive after nearly two years of this. Of hurting and bleeding. Of being repeatedly broken.

With two more brutal thrusts, he lets out a roar as he explodes inside of me. I feel nothing as he collapses onto me; with each dying jerk of his hips, the extent of the pain becomes apparent when it hurts even to breathe.

Sighing, he finally moves off me, and once his touch is gone, cold air nips at my sweat-soaked skin. It's cold, but I welcome it, needing to be numb.

"Fuck me," he gasps, collapsing on our bed. Turning, I take in the terrifying sight of his body through the strands of my damp hair. After nearly two years with him, he's still the same as when I first laid eyes on him. Just as lethal and feared, though perhaps a little rougher around the edges.

Licking sweat from his top lip, he lifts his hand and crooks his finger. My body tenses. *No.* No more. I can't—

"Come here." When I don't move, he cocks one eyebrow, and I know it's his way of silently asking if I dare go against anything he wants.

My body shakes as I rotate, using the wall to keep me upright as I face him. It wouldn't be the first time I've fallen after his attack.

Dark eyes devour me. I'm naked—his private exhibition. My scars and bruises his art. And he's proud. So fucking proud of what he's done to me.

Letting go of the wall, I stumble over to him when all I truly want to do is stab him. Grabbing my sore hips, he sits me on his lap and pushes my hair aside. "What will you do while I'm gone?"

"Nothing," I whisper as he puts tiny sick kisses along my jaw that only make my skin crawl.

"Oh?" He chuckles. "You're not going to dream of me, baby girl?"

Heat creeps up my neck. *Shit.* "Of course, Blake—"

His hand wraps around my neck, fingers clenching against my windpipe. Pulling me closer, he flicks out his tongue and licks me, leaving a trail of cigar-smelling saliva from my chin to my hairline. "You *better* dream of me, Heidi. Dream of me rolling in on my bike in a few days. I want to see you waiting and ready for me."

"Y-yes, Blake." I hope he crashes on his fucking bike and dies.

"Good girl." He shoves me off his lap. "Now, get me a drink. I got calls to make before I go."

Wiping spit from my face, I grab my housecoat from the floor and slip it over my shoulders, groaning from the ache in my bones. As I slip my feet into a pair of slippers, he starts talking on the phone. "Drop the guns off Monday. I'll be up in Dawlin this weekend, sorting shit out with that fucker Jerome. The boys left this morning. There's no one here, but Milton." He lights up another cigar and then stops, eyeing me. Dropping my gaze, I scurry out of the bedroom, and as I make my way through the club, I cringe at the state of it. The place is trash. Alcohol and stale smoke linger in the air from last night's party, empty bottles and overflowing ashtrays filling this pit that I call my prison.

There was a fight—a brawl between two men over a new girl named Florence. Like madmen, they couldn't seem to grasp that she is to be shared. Blake allowed the fight to go on longer than it should have for entertainment. It's made the place extra messy, tables and chairs toppled over, with sprays of blood on the floor.

I let out a sigh, knowing Nicole's meant to clean the place before Blake comes out and sees. He'll beat the crap out of her if it's not done, hard on her the most. After failing to give him the money owed for the heroine she took from him, he doesn't trust her.

I find her curled up on the floor passed out as I'm heading into the kitchen. Seeing her soaked in vomit with her panties twisted around her ankles drives that knife further into my heart. Because no matter what she did and how much I despise her, she's still my sister, and I hate seeing her like this.

"Nicole. Get up." I nudge her with my foot, and she groans. Still alive—though I'm not sure how with all the puncture holes from needles dotting her arms. An addiction she hid from me when she could have told me. I would have helped her.

"Fuck off," she slurs, drunkenly flapping out her arm, I think to hit me. Cracking her eyes open, she stares up at me blankly, not recognizing me. She never does when she's like this.

"You need to clean the place," I tell her, wishing I could be strong enough to let her stew in her filth and not care about her. She doesn't deserve it. Not by how she treats me—the drugs stealing her humanity and replacing her with a creature that would do anything for a shot of it.

"*You* clean it," she sneers, saliva dribbling down her chin. She doesn't even wipe it away. That's how much of a mess she is. Cruelly smirking, she adds, "*Princess.*"

So she *does* know it's me.

Squaring my shoulders from her taunt, I step over her and go into the kitchen, ignoring her cackling behind me. She won't follow. She can't even stand, and Blake will beat her before he leaves. Hopefully, bad enough that I won't have to see her for the weekend while she heals.

Shutting her out, I take my time making Blake's drink, not in a rush to go back to him. Pulling a glass from the cupboard, I mix him a Black Russian that Milton taught me to make. Blake will want something substantial for the journey to Dawlin—a small biker town miles out from Fair Haven.

A bottle of bleach next to the sink catches my eye and makes me wonder what would happen if I slipped some in his drink. I wish I knew. Not that I'd ever get away with it. Everyone would know it was me as I'm one of the only few Blake allows to get him a drink.

I go with the safer option, tipping in more alcohol to make it stronger, hoping it will increase the chances of colliding into something on his journey.

Morning at the club means emptiness and quiet. I appreciate this time of day when I'm usually the only one awake, and everyone else is gone. This weekend especially, will be bliss with Blake and the rest of them at the festival in Dawlin.

Not that I will be alone, as Milton's staying behind to watch me.

The sound of heavy footsteps thumps behind me as I twist the cap back on the bottle. I expect it's Milton, as he's usually never far away. But, when I turn and see Grady, Blake's fourth in command, anxiety squeezes my muscles.

I don't like him, not one bit. Older than Blake, with haggard features and wild gray hair, he wears a sneer on his face like he doesn't know any other expression. And I know he isn't supposed to be here. He should be almost arriving at Dawlin with the rest of them.

"Where's Blake?" he demands when he sees me.

"Bedroom," I answer, and step back when he closes the kitchen door, shutting us both inside.

"And Milton?" Something inside of me knows I should lie. "He'll be back in a second." A cold sweat breaks out over my skin as he stalks forward, cornering me in. "What are you doing?"

"Getting back what should be mine. May as well have my fun before taking out the big man, seeing as he keeps boasting about how tight your cunt is."

My head hits the counter and knocks the air from my lungs. When hearing the distinctive sound of his belt and zipper, I begin to struggle, scouring the counter for anything to stab or hit him with. I try grabbing the liquor bottle I was using, but it's just out of my reach, and I scream, "No!"

"Shut the fuck up," he hisses, holding me down and exposing my rear to him. Forcing his fingers unexpectedly inside of me, I squeal with horror from the intrusion. "So wet," he marvels. "Does this turn you on?"

My nails claw at the countertop as he kicks my legs apart, but just before he pushes himself inside, the door bursts open. "Where the fuck is my drink—"

Blake stands in the doorway, eyes sparking with fury as he takes in the scene. Growling out with anger, he's across the room in seconds and pulling Grady off me, bashing him in the face with his fist.

As Blake swings his fist to hit him again, Grady dodges and elbows him in the nose instead. My heart leaps when Blake stumbles back, blood spraying from his nostrils down his chin as if someone turned on the faucet to its highest setting.

Taking the opportunity, Grady moves fast, grabbing his arm and twisting it behind his back. Blake's knees buckle as Grady sneers, "You are over, Blake. We want you out of the presidency."

Blake laughs. "You mean *you* want me out."

Grady twists his arm again, and something cracks. Blake yells out in a way I've never heard before. "You've got more foes than you have allies under this roof. Even ones in your inner circle," he reveals. "You're driving this place to the ground with your wars and bloodshed. My father worked too hard to make Devil Horns *mean* something. You and that boy of yours aren't fit to lead."

MILTON: WORSHIP

A shadow appears in the doorway, and stomach flips when I see Milton aiming a gun at Grady's head. From this angle, he can't see him, but Blake does, and he sighs. "Should've killed me when you had the chance. Better luck in Hell, fucker."

Gunfire booms, and a bullet hits the side of Grady's face, then he crashes to the floor. I stumble back, horrified as blood forms a pool beneath him. Letting out a croaky laugh, Blake turns to Milton. "Where the fuck have you been?"

"The feds were on my ass," he says, stowing his gun away. "I had to divert."

Grabbing a chair for support, Blake heaves himself off the floor, clutching his chest as he does. Peering over his shoulder, he eyes me furiously. "You. Get here. Bring my fucking drink."

Shaking from head to toe, I grab his drink and go over to him, circling the dead man in the middle of the kitchen. Once I'm in reaching distance, he holds the glass and downs it in one swallow. Then he slams me up against the fridge. "You cheating on me, whore? Did he touch you?"

"Blake—"

"Did he *touch* you?" I sob, nodding, as he growls. "Where?"

"He put his fingers inside of me," I admit, tears once again drenching my face. I can't look at Milton, shame burning through me.

Blake's eyes go from disgust to anger. A dangerous series of reactions that make me worry about my life. "And did you like it?" I blink a few times in disbelief, glancing at Milton, who is staring at the floor. "Don't look at him. Answer me!"

"No!"

"I don't believe you." I gasp when he throws me at Milton, as he often does when he's had enough of the sight of me. Hands catch me as they always do, and I break into a sob, wishing this nightmare would end. Milton gives my shoulder a little squeeze. *Pull yourself together.* "Get her cleaned up and ready to leave in thirty minutes. You are both coming to Dawlin with me."

CHAPTER ELEVEN
TWO YEARS AGO

After taking the hottest shower and scrubbing Blake's taste from my mouth, I take in my reflection. My tiny denim shorts and the tight black vest Florence gave me to wear. The shorts just about cover my ass, and I know how Blake gets when I display my body outside of the club. He won't be happy with this.

Not that I have time to find a Blake-approved outfit, as I've heard him roar at Milton to hurry the fuck up. After calling her to help, Florence rushed my makeup and hair under Milton's instruction, and I'll admit, she did a fantastic job under the circumstances. You wouldn't even think there was anything wrong with me, that I was just an ordinary girl excited to attend her first festival.

As I slip my feet into a pair of knee-high boots and bend to tie the laces, Milton bursts into the bedroom. As always, my heart jumps to my throat whenever I see him, terrified, yet strangely liking his presence. He's the only one who has no interest in hurting me. I'm just his job, and while I find myself fantasizing it wasn't, I know this is reality. "You ready?"

My forehead creases at the thunder in his eyes. Eyes that make my stomach do somersaults sometimes. He's angry—something I rarely see. Probably Blake related, or I hope. Maybe he's mad at me. "Yes."

Dark eyes rake down my body as they often do, though there's never a hint of what he's thinking. I shouldn't *want* him to look at me. I'm not sure how old he is, but it's clear he's older, and if Blake caught him, he'd be dead in an instant. Turning, he stomps away, and I follow. We head outside, and I shield my eyes with my hand from the sun's glare I haven't seen in weeks.

"Took your fucking time," Blake complains. He's sat proudly on his silver Harley—his pride and joy. He's clutching the side of his ribs, expression contorted with pain as he glances over his shoulder to get a better look at me.

He observes my outfit, and my gut twists. "Come here."

Releasing me, Milton walks over to his bike as I go over to Blake. Once I'm near, his free arm snakes around my waist to pull me onto his monstrosity of a motorcycle. He traps me against the handlebars and sighs. "You look good."

My eyes briefly connect with Milton's, but he looks away as Blake massages my thigh. "Milton can't be killing people where we're going, babe. You stay with him and keep your fucking trap shut about what went down earlier."

That surprises me. I'm not sure why Blake wants to keep it a secret that Grady's dead. Wouldn't he want to tell the rest of them that he turned his back on them?

I nod, never asking questions, not wanting to.

Pinching my chin between his fingers, he smacks a disgusting kiss on my lips. It's slow and drawn out at first, eventually hardening. My stomach lurches, wishing he would stop. Finally, he does.

"You're riding with Milton." He shoves me off his bike and turns to him. "No stops. I want to get there before nightfall," Blake orders, putting his helmet on. Milton thrusts a smaller black one into my chest, and I grapple to catch it.

"Put it on," he says, shoving his own over his head. I put it on, my heart racing at the thought of getting on his bike. After securing the strap under my neck, Blake's Harley cuts through the courtyard. Gesturing some sign with his hand, he takes off.

"Get on," Milton demands, swinging his leg over the motorcycle. Apprehensively, I eye the dangerous black machine, my body shivering with nerves.

Stepping forward, I brace my hands against the seat and stretch my leg over the smooth leather padding. Once I'm on it, Milton locks his fingers around the backs of my knees and tugs me forward until I'm against his leather-bound back.

Heat burns my cheeks as he reaches back again, this time taking my arms and wrapping them around his torso. "We're riding fast," he warns. *"Don't let go."*

His foot slams down, and the engine roars to life. My teeth chatter from the rumble of the bike, and I've barely tightened my grip around him when we suddenly take off.

Oh. My. Fuck.

Wind smacks into my face, stealing every bit of air from my lungs. I cling onto Milton so tightly, he stiffens, like I'm hurting him. I can't help it. My stomach turns over, and I pinch my eyes shut as he turns a corner sharply. I expect any moment to fall off. I even wait for the impact of the ground.

It doesn't come, and when I open my eyes, we're now speeding down the highway, Fair Haven behind us. Milton's bike thunders as he picks up speed, dodging the rush hour mob. As cars thin out, I spot the sign to Dawlin. Getting braver, I peek over his shoulder. To my surprise, it's not as bad as I thought it would be. As my sight expands across the freeway, another bike rides in the distance ahead—the shade of silver hard not to recognize like its owner.

I can't believe my luck. What was supposed to be a weekend away from Blake has turned into one with him. Not to mention the unexpected of going to the place we are. I've never been out of Fair Haven in my life.

"How much longer?" I call out, risking talking to Milton, who has said nothing the entire time.

"An hour," he replies, and my shoulders slump. An hour seems like a long time.

Daylight fades fast, and it feels like more than an hour has passed before we come to the small, dusty town of Dawlin.

The buildings are ancient and not what I expect. Not from how everyone talks about this place like it's biker paradise. All I see is a dump.

Ahead, Blake takes a turn, and Milton follows. Ten minutes later, I hear something—rock music. Gazing over Milton's shoulder again, we quickly approach a field filled with rows of motorbikes and parked cars. Beyond them are hundreds of black tents and a carnival. Pulling into parking spaces side by side, Blake and Milton cut their engines. Milton says something, but I'm not listening, too busy soaking in everything. All the new. There must be hundreds of people here, a buzz of excitement filling the air.

"Heidi!" Blake snaps, and I turn to face him. He's off his bike, helmet removed, and sweat dripping down his face. He doesn't appear well as he holds out his hand to me.

Duty calls.

Climbing off Milton's bike, vibrations still ripple through me as I pull off the helmet and go over to Blake. Once I'm near enough, he grabs me and wraps his arm around my shoulder, leaning his weight on me. My legs, shaky from the ride, threaten to collapse. He's so fucking heavy.

"You want something for that?" Milton steps forward, fumbling inside his inner jacket pocket, his eyes like a forest on fire in the setting sun. His cheeks are flushed from the journey as mine probably are, his black hair mussed and damp from the helmet.

"What you got?"

"Something to help with the pain." He pulls out a small baggie of pills.

"Hit me up." Milton hands the bag over, and leaning off me, Blake fishes two out of the packet and swallows them dry.

"You might want to get yourself checked out when you get back. And Nick needs to know about Grady."

Blake nods, resembling the older man he is. "Fill him in when you're both alone. Fuck knows who the bastard's been talking to about our shit. Something's going on. We keep our heads down until I get this deal sorted with Jerome, then we seek out the traitors. I know there's more."

Nodding, Milton walks ahead, and Blake drags me along under his arm. He draws me closer just as we're about to enter. "Remember what I said. Say a word, and I'll put a gun in your pussy and pull the trigger. You hear me?"

"Yes, Blake." The threat drifts to the back of my mind as we pass through the entrance and into chaos. There are so many men and women, but no children, despite the Ferris wheel and other rides across the field. Cotton candy and hotdogs tease my senses, reminding me that I haven't eaten anything at all today. Knowing I can't rely on Blake to feed me, I make a mental note to ask Milton later.

Soon, we arrive outside a large tent, and as we walk inside, the Devil Horns logo greets us, alongside two others I don't recognize. Unlike back in the club, there's a chilled atmosphere here. Chatter and laughter fill the air instead of anger and testosterone.

Blake's men blend with faces I don't know, seemingly all having a good time. "It's neutral territory," Blake answers my unspoken question. "No one can do shit here."

"What the fuck is she doing here?" a voice suddenly rages.

It's Nicolas. He has a blond on his lap he's not the least bit interested in, and judging by the slur in his voice, he's drunk—which is never the best combination.

"Mind your own fucking business," Blake snarls, shoving me to the side.

Assessing his father, I know what Nicolas sees. The usual frightening calmness Blake emits is gone. He's agitated, in pain, and sweating profusely. "What's going on?"

"Nothing. Go back to your slut. We'll talk later."

Angered, Nick turns and leaves the gazebo. With a nod from Blake, Milton follows him, and I'm suddenly standing alone, not knowing what to do.

Someone hands Blake a beer, and he knocks it back. The pills Milton gave him seem to have kicked in as he isn't hunched over anymore.

Only Deuce joins us as they head over to a table. I trail behind, hearing Deuce say, "There's no sign of Jerome yet."

Blake grunts and sits. Snapping his fingers at me, he points at the seat next to him, and I sit. "He better not stand me up."

"Word's gettin' round that Skylar thinks you're gonna cause shit," Deuce adds, not that I know what, or who, they're discussing.

"Skylar can suck my cock. We all know he likes it," he grumbles, knocking back another beer.

"Where's Grady?"

My body tenses at the mention of him, but Blake doesn't have the same reaction, his expression normal. "How the fuck should I know?"

Deuce frowns. "He said he was riding up with you."

"Ain't seen him. You know how he is. Probably already here—face deep in pussy. Get me another beer, and if you see Jerome, send him my way."

Nodding, Deuce leaves, and once out of earshot, Blake pins me with the deadliest of glares I've ever seen him wear. "Next time, why don't you be more obvious."

I gasp when he grabs my leg beneath the table and squeezes so hard tears spring to my eyes. "Ow, Blake. Stop—"

"If it weren't for all these people, I'd bend you over this table and fuck some damn sense into you. Seeing as I can't, you better start acting like my fucking woman, or you'll be seeing an early death."

He lets go of me as Deuce makes his way back over with a round of beers. Just as he sets them on the table, Blake grabs one and lifts it to his mouth as my thigh throbs.

The words, *just kill me*, almost slip from my lips. I swallow them down and lift my gaze, my eyes locking with Milton's. I hadn't noticed his return, and I swear, as he turns to shield his expression from me, that I saw something I never have before—a look of anger toward Blake. I shake off the thought, knowing it's not true. Nobody cares about me. Especially not Milton.

CHAPTER TWELVE

The woman who greeted me in Milton's office yesterday enters the room moments after he leaves. I don't anticipate seeing her. Judging by how she carries herself with importance, she's not just a secretary like I first thought.

Again, she wears a black, conservative suit, her hair up, and the same shade of red lipstick coating her lips—yielding a powerful *don't-fuck-with-me* statement.

Wrapping the covers around me, her mouth stretches into a friendly smile. I know it's her way of attempting to calm me by her sudden appearance.

"Good morning." Well, at *least* she's more polite than Milton. "My name is Ms. Calderway, but you may call me Lisa if you wish. Mr. Hood wants me to accompany you back to Stonehill. I have new clothes for you to wear."

Lifting her arm, she showcases a white paper bag, likely expecting a thank you. I'd rather poke out my eye than thank her for getting me new clothes to replace the ones Milton destroyed. "Where's Milton gone?"

"A meeting." She smiles again, setting the bag on the end of the bed. This time, her lips hide something, and I immediately pick up the sense that perhaps she heard what he was doing to me just minutes before her appearance. "I will wait outside for you while you change. The shower is just through that door if you wish to take one." She points somewhere behind me. "Then we will be on our way."

After she leaves, I crawl to the end of the bed and pick up the bag. Peering inside, I scoff as I pull out a new set of Stonehill attire; the gray a little darker than my last ones, the fabric not as faded. At the very bottom are a pair of black panties and a matching bra, a tiny bit of lace trimming around the hem.

They're nice. Better quality than the ones I have on, and I know it's on purpose to embarrass me.

Climbing out of bed, groaning from the twinges of discomfort, I glance over in the direction Lisa had mentioned. A shower would be nice. Going inside a spacious bathroom, gold against black marble, I shuffle over to the large walk-in shower and switch it on.

Sighing as the spray hits my hand, I wait for the water to heat before stripping and stepping under the pressured spray. I sigh, not caring about my bandages getting wet as water cascades over my body, warming me. Making me feel like a fucking human.

Spotting a loofah and a bar of soap that smells like perfumed perfection, I rub suds into my skin, wincing as I rub between my legs.

Fuck Milton Hood.

After rinsing, I get a towel off the rack to dry myself and then get dressed. Lisa returns just as I'm putting on my sneakers, knocking on the door again before entering. "Are you ready?"

Nodding, I step out of the room, coldness impaling me when I come face to face with *that* door. The room Milton had me strapped to a bed for hours was opposite me all this time.

Heading back through the red tunnels, I trail after Lisa, soon reaching the foyer with the three arches. Not stopping, she goes straight for the door and opens it. When sunlight hits my face, my eyes sting. Although it's sunny, it's not warm. I shiver, spotting the car Milton used last night waiting for us.

Memories of him shoving me up against the side of it prod my mind, and I hate that my stomach dips at the thought of it. Of him.

As Lisa opens the back door for me, I peer over my shoulder at the imposing monstrosity behind me. Even in daylight, it's an enormous, ugly beauty, harboring secrets I don't think it wise to ever find out. Climbing into the car, I avoid eye contact as Lisa gets into the front and peels out of the driveway. Driving back through the isolated roads Milton took last night, my surroundings only become recognizable as we go over Fairdell Bridge. As the familiar buildings, half obscured beneath low misty clouds, come into view, it starts raining again, droplets slanting against the window as we make our way through the congestion of rush hour. Until, finally, we arrive back at Stonehill. My stomach coils at being back, wishing Milton had decided the best form of revenge was actually putting me out of my misery.

After getting out of the car, Lisa walks ahead, carrying a briefcase I didn't notice her having before. We pass security without question and then get into the elevator. Punching the second-floor button, we ascend, and once the doors slide open, we go down the corridor to the very end where my room is.

Lisa goes inside and I linger in the doorway, watching as she places the briefcase on the desk. Extracting a packet of documents and a pen from inside, she spreads them out neatly on the surface and turns to me. "I have a few things for you to sign," she tells me then.

"What is it?"

"A non-disclosure agreement. It needs to be signed for your relationship with Mr. Hood to continue. Everything is written down if you want to read, which might be wise. The clauses are quite specific."

"He wants me to sign a *gag order*?"

Her forehead creases. "We don't call it that. Did he not explain his desire for you to sign?"

"No." He seemed to have left that out entirely while he was torturing me. My wrists sting beneath the bandages, unable to believe this is happening, that he wants to put a muzzle on me after everything he's done to me.

"I'm sure he meant to. Nonetheless, by signing, you agree to not speak a word about your time spent with him and anything to do with Club X. It's non-negotiable. My client leads a diverse life." She shifts her weight onto the other heel when I still don't move. "Look, I don't ask questions. But if I can offer you any kind of security, other women have signed, and everything has been absolutely fine."

There's so much wrong with what she said that I don't know what to process first.

It slowly dawns on me that maybe this woman doesn't have a clue about the events that played out between myself and Milton. That the nature of what went on between us was glaringly different than those other women who signed.

"Once you do sign, you must have these on you at all times." She slides three things across the table as a further prompt. A mobile phone, an X card, and a small box. "It's mandatory until the contract between you and my client is terminated."

Finally, moving over to the table, I pick up the box, and when I open the lid, a silver ring taunts me from a velvet cushion. A silver X ring, though smaller. Delicate. Obviously, for a woman. "Did he give a ring like this to every female who signed?"

"Of course."

Anger bubbles inside of me as I incline my head toward the phone. "Can I call him?"

She eyes me cautiously before shaking her head. "No. If he wishes to contact you, he will. But you can't call him."

"Who's the tacky one now?" I mumble under my breath.

"Pardon?"

"How do I send him a message?"

"Through me," she answers proudly, as if controlling Milton's contacts makes her superior. "If there is ever an emergency, you call me. My number is already programmed in."

"Ok, well, I have an emergency now, actually, or not, I don't know." Stepping closer, Lisa instinctively leans back. Not that she's able to move very far, and taking that to my advantage, I capture the lapels of her jacket. She gasps with surprise, her brown eyes wide and startled. "What I do know is that it would be wise to tell Mr. Hood to go fuck himself. You're clearly misinformed about the nature of this so-called relationship between us. I'm not like his other bitches. If he wants to shut me up, tell him to come to do it himself. Unless he can't handle it. You got that?"

She nods frantically, her cheeks as red as her lips. "Y-Yes."

Letting go of her, I pick up the stack of papers and shove them into her chest. "Now, get out."

"But—"

"Get out!"

Shoving the documents messily back inside the briefcase, she leaves. The moment the door closes, a wave of dizziness has me falling to the ground.

Shit.

Pulling myself upright, I sit for a long time with tears spilling down my cheeks. The ache in my chest is so damn depressing. I don't know why my life is so fucked up. Pushing my fingers through my hair, I squeeze the roots and let out a violent scream, loud enough that one of the girls next door laughs at me.

"Shut up!" I yell at her, kicking my foot against the wall. She just continues laughing. Laughing. Laughing. Hugging my knees to my chest, I rock back and forth. It goes dark outside quickly, and the mobile Lisa gave me has rung out twice since she left. The nurses have long since finished their rounds, forcing me to take lots of little pills, all the while ignoring the phone and other things I shouldn't have on the table.

How silly of them to not question the items on my desk. I mean, there is the chance of swallowing the ring and choking myself to death...or rubbing the edge of the card over the cuts on my wrists until it slices through something detrimental.

What would they say then?

We didn't know she had them. She must've had someone smuggle them in.

Before I ponder further on that thought, the door opens behind me. No one is supposed to be here. It's after hours, and the door is meant to be locked, which makes me wonder if the nurses purposefully left it open.

With booted footsteps, such a sound shouldn't make something hot and sick spread through me. Yet here I am, feeling just that, my heart jumping to my throat as he says, "How do you want to do this?"

Hysteria bubbles in my chest, and I can't help laughing as I sense his presence behind me, deciding to taunt instead of adhering. Didn't he say I loved playing the victim? "Do what?"

"What I must do to shut you up." His irritated tone sends multiple shivers through me. "Is that not what you asked Ms. Calderway to tell me? To come to do it myself?"

"Thought I'd present you the opportunity to further be a *dick*."

Large hands grab my arms. Picking me up easily, he pushes me against the wall, pinning me from behind. I've yet to see his face, but I can imagine it. The spark of fury in his eyes drilling into the back of my head for baiting him.

I push back against him, bending my arm to jab him with the end of my elbow. Not that it does any damage, as all I hit is hard muscle. Keeping me against the wall with his hips, he grabs my arms and clamps them to my sides. "Get off me!"

"Stop fighting me. You don't want to wake up your neighbors and have them think you're having a bad dream…or a good one. You're a little messed up in that department, aren't you?"

"Fuck you." He turns me then, and I'm now facing him.

As I envisioned, his expression is one of fury, which I'm glad for. He's also wet from the rain outside, currently beating against the window. The droplets on his jacket seep through my shirt as his scent invades my nostrils—faded cologne and rain.

Donning a black leather jacket, dark jeans, and boots, the Milton I once knew has returned. Seeing him in his motorcycle gear takes me back to the multiple times he looked as he does now. Pissed. Frustrated.

All because of *me*.

"You almost gave Lisa a heart attack. Though, I guess I should have told her this wasn't a romantic endeavor."

"Then what is it?"

He shrugs nonchalantly. "You liked what I did too much."

"Do you honestly think I'd sign just so you can have another taste of me? I'm guessing those other women you put a muzzle on didn't quite match up, or you wouldn't be asking someone you hate to sign themselves over to you."

In the darkness, with moonlight pouring inside the room, his eyes are like pits of endless darkness as he glares at me. "I don't hear you denying it. And don't let my dick being hard fool you. Though I will admit to not expecting last night to end like that, and given your response, I'd say you didn't either. Sign and come with me now, or don't, and stay here to rot."

"And be owned by you?" I'm teetering along a perilous line, but I don't care. "There's no difference if I'm here, with you or Blake. And really, Milton, when do you throw a contract in front of a girl? Before or after dinner?"

"You almost sound…jealous." He captures my face with his free hand, and I fight a moan from his touch, losing the battle. I can't bear it. That he, of all people, is the one making me *feel* like this. "Bet you're wondering why all the secrecy? What could I possibly be doing to those women? Let's just say...I don't ever get complaints."

"You're revolting. I will *never* willingly give myself to you."

"And you are, once again, proving to me that you're not worth my time. However..." Stepping closer, his hand drops to my pants. Aware of what he's about to do, I slam my fists into his chest as hard as I can. Not that it seems to faze him as he loosens the strings of my pants and dips beneath the waistband. Once he's down, he pushes my panties to the side, sinking two fingers into me.

And I moan. I fucking *moan* for him.

The edges of my vision whiten as he brings forth what he left earlier today, sensations that make me want to do bad things. And I hate him. I fucking hate him. "You like this, and it changes things."

"It changes nothing." His fingers move, pushing inside of me slowly, causing my body to tremble all over again. "Call it my body's reaction, self-defense from sick assholes like you. I don't like you."

"And I don't like *you*. You are insufferable, and since you won't sign the fucking NDA, a liability."

I push my hips forward brazenly, deepening him inside of me. It almost tips me over the edge, but seeing confusion and anger in his eyes, makes it worth it. "The only liability around here is you. You could fuck my brains out, and I'd still feel nothing. Maybe a few years ago, I would have, but you gave me nothing. Not even when I worshipped the ground you walked on because I thought you were the only one who cared about me. How stupid I was, seeing as you only cared about your own agenda." He goes to pull his hand away, but I grab his wrist to keep him there. "So, correct me if I'm wrong, but you only want me to sign because it's *you* who likes doing this to *me*. Am I wrong?"

"Sign, and I might tell you."

"No."

"And here I was, willing to give you a chance to redeem yourself." This time he does pull away. Gasping, I slump against the wall, body throbbing. *Screaming.* He did it again, and I'm losing my mind, so turned on my panties are drenched. And he knows it.

Fuck, I want to cry. Hurt him.

Stepping back a little, he lifts his black T-shirt. At first, all I see is toned muscle. Skin that looks smooth in the moonlight. As my eyes follow the dark smattering of hair trailing down his naval, I spot it—a bullet-shaped scar just above his right hip. Lifting my eyes to his heated stare, I know exactly what that is. "Nick did shoot you."

"He did, thanks to you." He drops his T-shirt.

"How did you—"

"Survive?" He chuckles, but it sounds off. "Dima—a friend."

"I'm not apologizing," I say, even though the thought of him being shot because of my lies makes my stomach turn. "You want to punish me, then do your worst. But anything else..." Pulling scraps of energy from God knows where I lean off the wall and walk over to him. He stands still, teeth clenched behind his lips, but nothing else. Not even as my fingers skim against the front of his jeans, touching the solid erection bulging behind the material. Hard, as I knew he would be. "You're not getting from me."

He catches my wrist in his hand, and the side of his lip tugs upward, the green in his eyes catching fire. I wince when his finger grazes off the bandage, close to the healing wound, but it does nothing to stop the eruption inside my chest, my heart thumping hard and wild. "Don't tempt me." The British comes out more robust than it's ever been.

"I'm not." I jut my chin out defiantly. "I'm *daring* you." It's not me. This isn't what I do, but something about Milton wants me to break boundaries and rules. "And if you succeed in making my life more miserable than it is, *then* you can have me."

Breathing a heavy, slow sigh out through his nose, he lets go and takes a step back. Stopping by the table, he picks up all the items Lisa left behind. The phone, key card, and that damn ring. I'm shaking like a leaf and so dizzy, but I stand boldly as he takes enough steps back to reach the door.

"You might be sorry you said that," he says, giving me one last glance before walking out of my room. After listening to the last of his fading steps, all I can do is return to the corner of my room, his touch haunting my skin and his words ringing in my head.

You might be sorry you said that.

CHAPTER THIRTEEN
TWO YEARS AGO

As night descends, it brings forth a new kind of atmosphere at the festival. The air quickly changes from fun and relaxed to carnage and chaos. Music blares outside—some rock band the culprit that riles the crowd and injects crazy into every drunken soul in this strange place.

Smoke, beer, and bike fumes are all I smell—a sickening mixture that's making my stomach turn. Or maybe it's because of how out of control things are getting inside the tent.

I've never seen men so agitated and *desperate* as they fight over women who seem to love the attention and violence. It is quickly deteriorating into something potentially scary, and I'm nervous.

My eyes continue to rove over the crowd in search of Milton. I haven't seen him in a little while, and Nick hasn't returned at all. It's been just Blake and me for a time, having not left his side once even though I'm uncomfortable, exhausted, and in pain.

I can feel the bruises forming beneath the layers of makeup Florence covered me with from the events earlier today. I want more than anything to escape the crashing music and drunken men. Curl into a ball and sleep until all of this is over.

Not that I know where I'll be sleeping tonight. Blake hasn't mentioned anything about our sleeping arrangements, which worries me. I hope it's not in here with everyone else. I can only imagine how bad it's going to get in the next hour or two.

It's not safe here. *I'm* not safe here.

Blake's high and drunk, stewing in a haze of rage and whatever pills Milton gave him. Pills he took more of when it became evident that Jerome stood him up.

Not that it's stopped people trying to join him in the festivities. Regardless of his bad mood, beautiful women regularly saunter over to him to flirt. Because I'm here, he sends them out, and they leave with pouty lips while angling me with angry stares. Not that I care for their sickening jealousy. I'm doing them all a damn favor.

With each passing second, Blake's mood worsens. Any minute, he's going to pass out or tear this place apart. Two extremes that leave me vulnerable.

With Milton God knows where, I suddenly feel *unprotected.* And bursting to pee, having needed to go for the last three hours, but too scared to ask Blake if I can. When my stomach cramps, I know I can't hold it in any longer.

"Blake?" When he says nothing, I tap him on the arm. Grunting, he turns my way slowly, eyes bloodshot and half-closed.

"What?"

"I need the bathroom."

He snorts, slurring, "Hold it in."

"*I can't,*" I beg, close to tears. "I haven't gone all day."

Sighing, he waves his hand, slumping into the chair more. "Go. Come straight back."

What?

I hesitate, thinking he's joking, but when he waves his hand again, I jump up from the chair so fast my head spins a little. Although I know the protocol of going back to him when I'm done, with this new sense of freedom, my body itches to push boundaries. Break a rule or two.

No one looks at me as I push the chair back and quickly head to the exit. No one stops me as I cross the tent and go outside, all too busy to care about the blond girl leaving her master's side.

The roar of motorcycles battling it out on a track vibrates beneath my feet. The smells of hotdogs and cotton candy fill my senses, making my stomach twist with hunger. When was the last time I ate? Yesterday morning? I'm starving now and have no money to get food or even do anything.

Finding a row of unsanitary portable toilets, I relieve my bladder, hovering over the gross toilet seat to avoid sitting on it. After washing my hands, I go back outside.

Go. Come straight back.

I don't want to go back to the tent. I want to be out here. Though, instead of heading deeper into the festival, I find myself moving in the opposite direction, back at the entrance and staring out at the empty road.

What would happen if I ran? Right here and now?

The thought has my heart skipping a beat. Run or stay. Where would I go? How far would I get?

If caught, the punishment will be worse than anything I've ever endured. The ultimate betrayal. Who knows what Blake would do to me?

But then, how much longer can I continue living this life when I'm already slipping away? It could be my only chance

I take a step forward and fear floods my chest. It almost pushes me back, but I force myself forward.

Before I know it, I'm running. Wind whips through my hair, tears spilling over my eyelids. I'm crying. Panting. *Panicking*.

It clings to every part of me, screaming no, no, *no*!

It feels like I'm being chased. As if at any moment someone's going to reach out and grab me. Drag me back. Snitch on me.

No one does. There's no one around, only me and the noise of my feet pounding into the dirt. I run until the music is just a series of dull thumps in the distance, and the air changes to earthier tones; pine and damp moss.

A sharp burn in my lungs warns me to stop, and I slow to a walk, clutching the stitch at my side and breathing heavily into the night.

Surrounded by pure blackness, I can hardly see what's in front of me, and it dawns on me that I didn't think this through. My fear hasn't gone away. There's no relief. The further away I get, the worse I feel, until I'm questioning what the fuck I'm doing.

I've no idea where I am, and if I'm lucky to get out of here, it's not as if I can go to Mom with her being in Paris with Lawrence. Dad's out of the question, knowing for sure he will only march me straight back to Blake the moment I got home.

I have no one to go to and no way of getting out of Dawlin. I don't even know *how* to get back to Fair Haven. Even though I never thought I'd have this opportunity, I should have paid better attention to which directions we took.

I'm a fucking idiot.

Sickness swirls through me, and I stop walking. Dry retching, I bend over to get sick, though seeing as my stomach is already empty, nothing comes up. Straightening my back with a groan, I swipe tears and makeup from my face, knowing what I'm doing is a bad idea and will get me nowhere but sent to the Hill.

A burst of emotion rips through me, and I scream out pent up bitterness and frustration, loud enough birds scatter in fright from a tree nearby.

I want to be free more than anything, but this feels all wrong.

It's not fair. Not right. It's not so simple as finding the nearest police station and begging for help. How many times have I heard of girls being turned away and unbelieved. Returned to their abusers for an extra bit of cash in their pockets? Back to the criminals, they should be locking up instead of feeding. And I know Blake has "friends" on the inside that will do just that.

I take a step back, knowing it can't be like this. My escape needs planning. Leaving fate to chance isn't going to work. I *know* that.

Just as I'm about to turn around, the roar of a motorcycle rumbles behind me. Whirling around, I spot a lone headlight darting toward me, blinding me as it skids and stops before me.

As the light turns away and I see who it is, my stomach somersaults at a very pissed off Milton. "Are you on a death wish?"

"I...I needed the toilet." His jaw clenches at my lie.

"Get on the fucking bike, Heidi," he orders, never having said my name out loud before. "*Now.*"

Making my way over to him like the obedient bitch I've been trained to be, I grab the sleeve of his leather jacket and pull myself up behind him. After securing my arms around his waist, he stiffens, and I wonder why. "You're lucky I found you and not anybody else. If anyone knew Blake's girl—"

"I'm *not* his girl," I spit icily. "Are you going to tell him?"

"I should." Panic threatens to tip me off the bike. If Milton tells on me, I'll be dead. There's no doubt about it. A bullet will be put straight between my eyes, and Blake will kill Nicole and my parents out of rage. Wipeout my entire bloodline because he's *that* sick.

I grab Milton's sleeve again, and he glances over his shoulder at me. Being this close to him, with moonlight spilling down on us both, I never truly appreciated how…beautiful he is. Almost as if he's not meant to belong in this world. "Please, Milton, I know you don't like me, but don't tell him."

"Why do you think I don't like you?" he asks, which I'm not expecting. He's never really engaged in a conversation with me. I guess we're both breaking the rules tonight.

"I just know," I reply, unable to put it into words. The way he looks at me sometimes—like I'm a problem.

"Maybe in another life…things might've been different," he mumbles. Turning away from me, he revs the engine and takes off. Taking me back to Blake.

CHAPTER FOURTEEN

Gabriella visits me early the next morning. It's unusual and something I expect to be the cherry on top of this disaster of a week.

I tried to refuse to see her when learning of her arrival. After what happened last time, I'd rather avoid her as much as possible. Not that my refusal sat well with Vera, who told me she insisted on seeing me over an important matter.

I should have told her *important* typically means *dramatic* in Gabriella's language.

As I stroll into the cafeteria and spot her sitting at the table wearing the finest ensemble and sparkling like the Eiffel Tower, I want to turn and walk back out. She spots me before I can retreat, waving me over.

Knowing I have no choice but to suffer her annoying presence today, I go over to her, cringing when she assesses me. "You look dreadful. And what happened to your wrists?"

Sitting down, I tug my sleeves down to cover the bandages. "Tried to slit them with a plastic knife at dinnertime."

Reaching out, I grab the coffee I know she won't drink and down it. It's lukewarm and disgustingly bitter, but I need it if I'm going to survive not strangling her to death during this conversation.

"Oh, Heidi," she says, her eyebrows pulled together irritably. "Don't be disturbing."

Her being here bright and early is disturbing *me*. "I fell off a chair, don't be dramatic."

"Ashley is back tomorrow. I will see to it she sees you immediately. You're getting worse." *Great.* Just what I need. "Don't look so bored. There is a reason for my visit. A serious matter, in fact, as you are invited to the wedding after all."

My eyes narrow suspiciously. "I thought I was disinvited?"

"Well…" Her face is tight. "Elise wants you there. She's insisted… And what princess wants, princess gets." There's sourness to her tone, and I know it's because Elise has her daddy wrapped around her finger. Much to Gabriella's chagrin, as this is one competition she will never win.

As for being invited to the wedding, I can honestly think of nothing worse than attending the event with her ratbag fiancé, Scott.

"Lawrence wants me to make it clear to you that if you ruin the day in any shape or form, that will be the end of it, and you will be on your own." She pauses before revealing the next bit. "Elise wants you to be her bridesmaid."

I lean back in my seat. "What?"

"Believe me, I'm just as shocked as you are. But since it's her big day, it's imperative that she's happy. You *will* be her bridesmaid and tell her you're delighted that she's asked you to be part of the wedding." Funny how she doesn't want me in her world, yet her stepdaughter does. What a predicament for us both. "It was Scott's idea. Another reason for you to agree. His family is worth millions." My back stiffens, but she doesn't notice my reaction.

Fucking Scott.

Elise's fiancé is rich, gorgeous, and a demon. One time, not that long ago, I had to be *nice* to Scott Link. It was Elise's twentieth birthday, and she had extended the invitation to me. I didn't want to go, but Blake forced me, telling me to go and spend some time with my mother and the new family I hadn't seen in forever.

Even now, the details are blurred, but seeing Gabriella's life had tipped me over the edge.

During the years spent with Blake, I'd clung to the hope that she was working on getting me out, as she told me when I was younger. Though, as I walked through the door and saw her dressed in a form-fitting silver gown, so beautiful and radiant, something had shattered inside of me.

Because I'd been holding onto a lie.

While mingling with guests, her hand proudly placed in the crook of Lawrence's arm, her smile dropped when she saw me. Excusing herself from Lawrence and his friends, she rushed over and grabbed my arm.

"What the *hell* are you wearing?" she hissed venomously, pulling me upstairs and down the hall. "You look like a whore."

I was wearing a black dress with heels. I knew it was short, but it was the best item in my wardrobe of other terrifying outfits. We ended up in Elise's bedroom, leaving me standing in the middle of the room, she yanked open the closet.

"I'm sorry," I muttered, not able to comprehend how much of a stranger she was to me then. How...distant.

She wasn't trying to get a life for me. Us. She was living in it by herself and had been for a while. "Wipe that lipstick off your face and put this on." She shoves something at me, but I can't look down to see what. "When you come downstairs and meet Lawrence and Elise, do not tell them about the...*way* you live or *who* you live with. If they ask, you were living with your father, who kept you from me as punishment for leaving him."

She was about to walk away when I asked, "What about Nicole?"

She stopped in the doorway and glanced over her shoulder at me, her response was so detached I wondered where the hell my mother had gone. "Who is Nicole?"

With that, she walked out, leaving me staring after her with my heart on the floor. And I knew she was no longer the mother I knew.

As I was about to unzip my dress, there was a knock. A young man with hair the color of sand and light eyes barged in before I could tell him I was in there.

"Oh." He stopped when he saw me standing in the middle of the room. "I'm sorry. I was looking for my girlfriend. This is her room."

I swallowed, my throat closing in, not knowing what to say or do. "Um..."

His eyes searched my face, as if he were trying to figure out something. "You look familiar. Have we met?"

"No," I replied, my heart beating in my chest as he took a step into the room. "I'm...I'm Gabriella's daughter. I lived with my dad."

"Right." He clicks his fingers. "You're the girl Elise was talking to me about. Hannah, is it?"

"Heidi," I replied, cheeks flaming.

"I'm Scott, Elise's boyfriend. Have you met her yet?"

"N-no." I shook my head. "I only arrived. I was just changing."

"Why?" His eyes skimmed my body in a way that made my stomach coil. "I think you look much better in that dress." My head bowed to focus on the ground. I didn't hear his footsteps on the soft carpet until I saw his shoes. Then his finger was beneath my chin, lifting my head. He licked his lips and smiled again. His eyes were so light. So *blue*. "In fact, I think you look rather sexy." My face seared. "But I suppose we don't want the birthday girl's new little sister showing her up. Here, let me help you get changed."

I pulled away. "No."

"Why?"

I couldn't swallow, knowing this was wrong. "I should go—"

"Wait." He grabbed my arm before I could walk away. While his grip wasn't tight, it stopped me from leaving like I should have. "It's okay. We'll be family one day, and family *helps* each other. You wouldn't want to upset Elise after kindly inviting you tonight, would you?"

"We can't," I whispered, wanting to tell him it would be dangerous if he touched me. Wanting to tell him that there would be a target on his back. Consequences.

But I didn't.

I tried hard not to think of Elise, a stranger to me, as he took my hand and pulled me out onto a balcony. I tried not to think about what I was doing as he pulled the curtain across to hide us if someone were to walk into the room. I knew what was about to happen, yet I didn't run. Didn't stop it.

His hands found the straps to my dress, his touch sending shivers down my spine. I was cold; the cool, nighttime breeze ghosted my skin on the secluded balcony. He took his time taking my arms out of the straps, and once they were free, pulled down the top of my dress, exposing my breasts.

He sucked in a breath. "Where did you come from?"

My shoulders trembled as he placed his hands on the tops of them. It wasn't a nice feeling when he squeezed them, tweaking my nipples until they were solid.

He pushed me down to my knees, and I let him. Watched him as he undid his pants, eyes clouded with desperation.

Gabriella called me a whore, and this is what whores did. This is what she thought of me when she looked at me. Maybe it was time I acted like one.

"I promise I'll tell Elise how nice you are being." He breathed out, stroking his cock inside his boxers. He thought I was naïve. Stupid. That I didn't know this was manipulation. He had no idea that I had surpassed any stage of being groomed. Abuse knew my body well, and as he fisted my hair and pulled me toward his tiny dick, I let him shove himself into my mouth.

As it did often, my mind melted away from the act. An expert by now. *What she thought of me.* Though, I didn't have to put much effort into it, as only a minute or so later, he let out a choked sound as he came, ejaculating into the back of my throat, moaning. "Oh, fuck, yes."

Then it was over, and as I fixed myself, the sly smile on his face only revealed the truth I knew to be true. That there were sick people even in this world. The one my mother threw me away for.

There was part of me that *wanted* Milton to burst through that door and gun Scott down like some dark guardian angel. He'd call Blake, who would ride down here, only to see me on my knees with another man's seed thick in my throat. He would spit on Scott's dead body, but the fury he'd have for me would've been my main goal.

He'd put the tip of his gun against my temple, pull the trigger, and the nightmare would be over.

But none of that happened.

After tucking himself away, Scott left me on the balcony and returned to the party. I felt *dirty*. Disgusting. There was no Milton. No Blake about to kill me. I was just the whore they molded me to be. The *perfect* victim...and I was sick of it.

Days blend together since Milton left, and nothing has happened. I come to the realization then that maybe he's not coming back at all and was just making me think he was so that I'd torture *myself*.

I should be relieved, yet there's an emptiness inside of me that's too hard to ignore. He's gone, and I hate him for it.

Another morning arrives, and sunlight beams inside my room. The human alarm clock next door has been wailing since seven. Every day at seven. She then woke the psychopath opposite of me, who screamed at her to shut the fuck up, or she would rip her throat out. While usually, both would irritate me, I'm distracted, my mind haunted by the man who has always been an enigma since the moment he walked into my life.

Flipping onto my back, I pull the blanket over my face to shield the brightness. Although it's November, my room is like a sauna this morning with the central heating and sunlight. There's no air, and my body aches from the heat.

Grabbing the end of my nightdress, I scrunch it between my legs, trying to ease the pulse there. But the material chafes against me, and I groan from how nice it unexpectedly feels. Licking my dry lips, I squeeze tighter, and gasp.

"Do it." His voice punctures my thoughts. And while I know he's not truly here, I imagine he is. Lifting my dress, I run my finger along the top of my panties, throbbing for me to touch myself. To *relieve* whatever he started. *"Go on. You know you want to."*

Slipping my fingers down my panties, I moan as I touch myself, surprised by how slick I am. How wet. Grazing my fingers over my clit, I focus on the area Milton was licking before pushing two fingers inside of myself.

I whine, my insides soaking and hot. *"There you go. Now come for me."*

Biting my bottom lip, I do what I did again. Circling my clit and pushing my fingers inside of me. Each time, I go deeper, the pleasure building.

I think of Milton. Think of what it would be like to kiss him, his lips against mine. Hands touching me like I wanted him to do all those years ago.

My skin dampens as I tug the button of my dress open and touch my breast, gasping when I twist my hard nipple in my thumb and finger.

I'm close…just a little…more—

"Morning, Heidi." The door flies open with a thud, and I yelp in shock. Quickly pulling my hand away from between my legs, I poke my head out from beneath the cover. Vera stands in the doorway, taking in my tousled state with her eyebrow raised. "It's only me. Time to take your meds."

"Right." I'm flustered and embarrassed as I sit up. Ignoring the violent ache rippling my core, I take the tablets and a cup of water she gives me. Putting them in my mouth, I swallow them down after taking a gulp of water, just wanting her to go away so I can die from embarrassment.

"You have a meeting in half an hour," she says, jotting something down on her iPad before leaving. When I know she's gone, I fling myself back down on my bed and breathe out in frustration.

Fuck sake. The only thing I've done is made myself worse.

Eventually, pulling myself out of bed, I get dressed. I'm uncomfortable and need a cold shower, but I won't have time. After eating a quick breakfast in the cafeteria, Vera comes for me again, taking me to Dr. Rogue's office. My heart sinks when I see her as I walk inside her brightly lit office.

"Heidi." She smiles that annoying fake smile that makes my insides clench with hate. She's sat in her usual fancy chair, perfect as ever, wearing all white. "It's good to see you again. Come in."

Walking inside, I take a seat, something she's shocked by. So am I. Since when do I make it easy for her?

"How are you?" All I can do is stare at her, the painting I hate taunting me from the wall. I try my best not to look at it, scared of what I will see this time.

Instead, I watch as she grabs her stupid pen and begins writing down shit in a brand-new folder with my name on it. "What are you writing?" I ask darkly. "That I'm not paying attention?"

She lifts her gaze to look at me and laughs, "Of course not. Just observations."

"And what are those?"

She breathes out through her nose. "Have you been sleeping?" She knows I don't unless I can't help it. "Are you angry with me? I apologize that I haven't been here for you. My father's not doing too well. Terminal cancer. But I'm here now, and you can tell me why you're having trouble sleeping."

She shared with me, so she thinks I'll share with her?

"Why do you think?"

"I don't know; I'm not a mind reader, unfortunately. Maybe you could tell me?"

"I'd rather die." It comes out without me realizing it. A slip of the tongue. *I said too much.*

Her brow furrows as silence parades around us. Finally, she clears her throat. "Right, okay. Well, I guess that's all for today." Her smile is strained. "If you need anything, you know where to find me."

CHAPTER FIFTEEN

That night there's a storm. Violent wind rips through the building, rattling the bedroom doors, as if someone were trying to get in. Thunder bangs in the sky, instantly followed by a flash of light that whitens the room. Rain begins, heavy and loud, battering against the roof and my window.

It's sometime past one in the morning. Security finished their rounds five or so minutes ago. I'm wide awake and restless, but not because of the storm.

The shame of touching myself while thinking of Milton thickens in my throat. How could I have let that happen? How? And now I can't stop thinking about that stupid contract he wants me to sign, the worst part being I want it to be more than him making me pay for what I did to him. I want to know what it feels like to be with Milton Hood.

I don't know why. I'm psychotic for entertaining the idea. Sick in the head. Deserving of being here. I'm consumed by a man who cares less about me, wanting his return when all he wants to do is torture me.

I'm sick, sick, sick.

Tossing on to my other side, frustrated by my thoughts, something catches the corner of my eye. As I look up to see what, my heart stops at the dark form in the doorway. Just as I'm about to open my mouth to scream, it rushes forward, and a hand crashes against my lips.

"Shh," Nicolas hushes as my eyes widen. Something cold presses against my throat and I whimper behind his palm at the blade on my skin. "Don't give me a reason to hurt you, free bird."

It's been months since I've seen him, and time hasn't been kind; he looks awful. Cuts tarnish his swollen face, blackening in areas where bruises have formed. Ashy hair falls around his shoulders now, wet from the storm and dripping water on my face. He looks every bit of the man Blake abused him to become. "I'm going to remove my hand, but if you scream, I'll cut you. Understand?"

Nodding, he takes his hand away slowly. Warily. When I don't scream, he relaxes, lessening the pressure on the knife against my throat.

"Daddy misses you," he taunts with a smirk, the weight of his body smothering me. He smells of alcohol and smoke, and he's *here*. How the fuck is he here? "We're bringing you home soon."

My head shakes, "No—"

"You *will* come home if you want to keep that little murderous secret you have to yourself." He sighs when I gasp. "That's right, I know all about what you did. I've been watching you all this time, knowing how that mama of yours made all the bad things her daughter did go away."

"Wh—what?"

"Did you get my present?" he asks, evil pouring into his gaze.

My head flinches back, tears welling in my eyes when he flashes me a cold smile of deviousness. "It was you. You dug up my baby." His eyes squint harshly as my stomach churns. "I didn't know I was pregnant, I…" Had a headache. Didn't want to be alive anymore. Tried to kill myself. I couldn't live with the guilt of betraying Milton any longer. Which one to tell him? "Does he—"

"No. But he will if you make this difficult for me. You know he's wanted to put a baby in you for years to replace the *damaged* one," he spits, talking about himself. "If he *ever* found out, he'd kill you, and you know it."

"I'm…"

His hand goes around my neck, and fear coats my insides as his fingers close around my throat. "Fuckin' cunt. Do not say you're sorry. You're not sorry. I can't stand the damn sight of you. Nothing but a dirty whore!"

"Nick, I can't…I can't breathe…" His hand clenches tighter, crushing my windpipe and blocking out air. Kicking out my legs, I slap his hands, trying to get him to stop.

"I'll come for you during the wedding. Blake wants you back where you belong." I smack his arm frantically. I can't breathe. I'm going to die! "Since you got yourself locked up in a psych ward, you're protected, and the wedding is the only opportunity, so be ready to come without a scene…And Heidi…"

He leans in so close I'm not only being strangled, I'm being crushed by his weight. "Don't even think about getting anyone to help you. Because I will kill them all."

Finally, he lets go, and I inhale loudly, coughing when air fills my lungs too fast. Placing my hand over my chest, I look up, still gasping, my room now empty, and Nick long gone.

I PACE MY ROOM ALL NIGHT, UNTIL THE FIRST TRACES OF DAYLIGHT uncover another stormy day, which seems to only add to the impact of Nick's sudden arrival.

My hands grasp the sides of my head, heart palpitating, and stomach cramping with nausea. No. This isn't happening. It *can't* be. I have to get out of here. There's no way I can go back to Blake. I *can't*.

As my thoughts swirl too fast in my head, only one person comes to mind. There's only one who can help me.

Opening the door, I rush down the corridor to the nurses' station. My fist pounds on the door, but there's no answer. Moving around to the other side and peering through a gap in the curtains, I spot all the nurses chatting over tea and coffee. I bang on the window angrily, and one by one, they turn to me.

It's Vera who gets up and opens the door. Hooded eyes reveal tiredness, her nightshift almost over. "Why aren't you asleep. You can't have any more medication, Heidi."

"I don't want pills," I snap impatiently. "I need to see Milton Hood."

She cocks an eyebrow. "Who?"

Is she kidding me?

"Milton Xavier Hood," I repeat, pronouncing his name slower. "He has an office on the other side of the building." I point down the corridor. "You took me to him the before, don't you remember? I need to speak to him. Tell him it's urgent."

She scratches her head. "I don't know who you are talking about." Turning to the other nurses, she asks, "Do any of you know a Milton Hood?"

They all shake their heads.

"He's here," I say, exasperated that nobody seems to know who the fuck he is. "I will take you to his office right now if you let me go through those doors—"

"That side of the building has been closed down for fifteen years, Heidi." I blink in shock. Disbelief. "Come now, it's early. You should still be in bed. I will send a message to Dr. Rogue in a couple hours if you really have to speak to someone."

"No!" I shout louder than intended. This is ridiculous. There's no way I imagined him. Lifting my hand to wipe the sweat from my forehead, I sigh, "Please just listen. I don't want to see Dr. Rogue. I want Milton Hood. He's the only one who can help me. Please. Maybe if you contact Lisa, you'll find him."

"Lisa, who?"

"Calderway. She said if I ever needed to contact him, I contact her first."

"Heidi," Vera breathes, stress evident in her tone. "I really wish I could help you, but I swear I don't know who you are talking about. Come now, I'll bring you back to your room myself. You can watch some television."

She tries to take hold of my arm, but I move back a few steps. "This is bullshit, Vera, and you know it. You know who I'm talking about…" I trail off, something reminding me of a particular gag order he tried to have me sign.

"Did he have you all sign that NDA?" She looks right through me. "He did, didn't he? You signed—you all did, and that's why you can't talk about him."

I laugh. Of course. How could I be such an idiot? And Vera here is in the wrong profession. What a terrific actress. But, of course, she shakes her head. "We didn't sign anything. Come on, back to your room."

"Stop making me out to be crazy!" She goes to grab me, and her hand catches my arm, but I pull away. "Why aren't you listening to me?"

"Calm down this instant," she scolds, taking hold of my arm again. "There are sick girls in bed who are resting. You are going to disturb them."

"You don't fucking understand!" Hot tears of frustration tumble down my face. "I have to speak to him. I need—"

Two other nurses join Vera to help, while others watch from afar. "This isn't like you, Heidi," one of the nurses says. "If I knew who this man was, I'd get him for you."

I snort in her face. "No, you wouldn't. You don't give a shit. Nobody in this fucking place gives a shit!"

Vera steps forward and points down the corridor. "Back to your bedroom. There's nothing we can do for you here. I will make sure you see Dr. Rogue later."

That's it.

I go for her, wanting desperately to get my hands around her neck. Before I can even touch her, two male orderlies that must've been sneaking up behind me grab me. "Get the hell off me!" I shout, bucking my body from their grabby hands. "You're all damn liars! He's real, and you know it!"

They drag me down the corridor, kicking and screaming, and put me into my bedroom. After dumping me on my bed, Vera and the brunette nurse enter. As hands hold me down, I scream when Vera holds up a syringe with a clear liquid inside—like something out of a godawful horror movie. Leaning over, she drives it into my vein, and she's not gentle about it. It stings as she presses down the plunger, injecting me with poison. "He's real," I sob, the room getting hazy.

Sleepy. I'm sleepy…

Then the room fades to black.

CHAPTER SIXTEEN

They up my medication—an array of colorful tablets emptied down my throat twice a day to keep me subdued and unable to get out of bed. They stripped me of privileges and took my choices. All because I lost control. Had a meltdown.

The dose is strong, forcing me to be relaxed and tired. So *tired*. I drift in and out of consciousness, floating in an endless sky of clouds.

I think Dr. Rogue visits me at some point. What day or time I have no idea. Just know that she said things to me.

This is for your own good.

You're going to be just fine.

Gabriella doesn't come. Maybe they told her I have the flu or something. Who knows? They lie. Every single fucking one of them in this stupid place is a *liar*. All because I asked to see someone they know is real.

I don't stop asking for him despite it making the situation worse. I *never* stop. They ignore me, roll their eyes at me, and tell me

Milton has to be a figment of my imagination, which I made up for attention.

The more I ask, the more they sedate me. God only knows how much time has passed. A few days. Weeks. Maybe a month. And while I'm stuck like this, the clock ticks down the days until I'm marched back to the club by Nicolas. When I'm taken back to my monster.

I'm not strapped to my bed, but I might as well be. I'm unable to leave my room, my bed. My clothes get tugged from my body without permission. I'm naked in front of men and women who wash me down with a rough cloth and slather me in sickly sweet soap. They toilet me and spoon feed me and keep the same cartoon channel on the TV.

When the skies outside my window dim and shadows come out to play, I'm fifteen all over again, being held down and raped by Blake. Being fucked to an inch of my life by Blake. Being tortured and beaten by *Blake*. Until I'm waking up screaming, drenched, lashing out at those trying to calm me.

And the only one I call for is the one who doesn't come. Milton.

The morning after my latest episode, they get me out of bed to have my session with Dr. Rogue. I go by wheelchair, and if that isn't bad enough, in an ironic twist, they wheel me right past *those* double doors before leading me to her office.

Dr. Rogue is standing by the window, gazing out at Fair Haven with a smile on her lips. She looks distracted. Happy.

Turning to face me, her smile wavers, like I'm the terrible smell under her nose. "Hello, Heidi. How are you?" I don't reply as the tech locks the wheels of my chair and leaves. Making her way over to her desk, she picks up my folder to write more notes down about me. Probably something along the lines of being *uncooperative. Unresponsive.*

She takes her seat in front of me and crosses her leg. When she finally points her gaze in my direction, eyes scanning me, I stare back at her, heart thumping with anger. Hate. Then she breathes a laugh. "Please don't look at me like that."

"Like what?" I croak, voice raspy from not using it.

"Like I'm the worst person in the world." She wets her lips with her tongue. "Despite what you believe, I want you to get better. Such a beautiful girl shouldn't be in a place like this." She's patronizing me. *Bitch.*

"I'm *not* lying," I whisper. "He's real."

Her head shakes, and she jots down more shit. "Why is it you want to see this person so badly?"

"You wouldn't believe me even if I did tell you."

"Try me."

I hold up my wrists. "Ask me how *this* happened."

"I know how that happened. You did it to yourself. We have an incident report of a nurse walking in on you scraping your wrists on the corner of a table. You'd been doing it for hours."

"That's not—"

"I know I can't possibly relate to the things you have been through in your life, and I know it's been so difficult for you. But this lying has to stop."

"But I—"

"No interruptions, please. I am unfortunately running out of options. You're getting increasingly worse. You're aggressive toward staff, self-harming, and you talk about dying. We might have no choice but to move you to a different facility with even tighter restrictions."

"You're twisting everything I'm saying!" Emotion clogs the back of my throat.

"You're not helping yourself." She gets out of the chair and makes her way over to me. Tears burn the rims of my eyes as she places a manicured hand on my shoulder, crouching in front of me until we're eye-level. "I want you to get better. I want to see you leave this place, as does your mother." She squeezes my shoulder, and all I want to do is grasp her neck until it breaks. "But this is not the way to go. Everyone is worried."

"I'm not making Milton up," I growl. "He's *real*. I can take you to him if you just let me."

"Don't get upset. It's okay to want attention—"

"I'm not doing this for attention," I argue, exasperated at her attempt of turning this on me.

"I know your relationship with your mother is strained and has been for a while. Elise is getting married to a wonderful man and has a great life. Something even *I* am envious of. Your mother has been occupied with the wedding and hasn't been able to give you much attention. It's okay to want her attention, Heidi. At least you have a mother who cares about you."

My body shakes with violent rage that seems to have exploded from nowhere. How far up Gabriella's ass she must be to think everything I have done is because I want attention from her?

She's the one who's fucking insane. The one who should be sitting in this wheelchair. "You have no idea what you're fucking talking about," I say through gritted teeth. "I fucking *hate* her."

Her eyes lower with disdain. "You shouldn't speak of hate like that."

I glare at her, wanting so much to scratch her eyes out. "*Yes,* I hate her. She's a lying bitch who left me with a rapist when I was a *child* while she was off exploring the world. You can't help me, *Ashley*, so please, shut the fuck up!"

Her hand suddenly whips through the air and crashes against my face. *Smack!* The pain is sharp, the noise loud, but the silence that follows is quiet.

My cheek smarts—a bruise already rising. The mask she had in place is gone as she straightens her back and strokes the side of my face where she hit me. I cringe from her touch.

"I will prescribe some painkillers for that," she says calmly, smoothing down her blouse. "Our session is over for today."

CHAPTER SEVENTEEN
TWO YEARS AGO

A week has passed since being in Dawlin, and we're back at the club. Blake went to the hospital after our return, the injuries Grady inflicted far worse than he thought. Three broken ribs and a fractured wrist. He was given medication and told to rest, which for once, he did. He hasn't touched me since, and I'm glad because my own body gets a chance to heal from his brutality.

It wasn't even an hour back when Milton was ordered to run an errand for Blake on his bike. He hasn't been here all week, and while I don't know why, his absence has my insides knotting. Because Milton holds a secret that could annihilate me.

He didn't rat me out to Blake for attempting to run. He didn't march me back by the scruff of my neck and reveal Blake's dutiful whore tried to leg it the first chance she got. That night, he didn't return me to the gazebo, where Blake and his motley crew were causing anarchy.

He took me to a campsite. A vast grassy field that was full of black tents in rows. Parking near the outskirts, furthest away from the festival itself and drunks making a ruckus, he'd shoved a sleeping bag at me from the compartment inside his bike.

His eyes grazed the area meticulously, though no one was around. The temperature had dropped, and my body shivered as I clutched the sleeping bag against my chest. Turning, he pulled another small bag from his bike and handed it to me. Using the headlight from his motorbike that was still on, I sighed in relief when fresh clothes sat inside—a long-sleeved black shirt, leggings, clean underwear, and fluffy socks.

"Florence," Milton explained, and I made a mental note to thank her when I got back. "You can dress in that tent there." He pointed to one behind me.

Nodding, I bent down to untie the laces on my boots, leaving them outside before peeling back the curtain of the tent and stepping inside. It was dark, though I managed to find a battery-powered lamp in the corner and switched it on. I got undressed awkwardly, not able to stand, the roof of the tent not high enough.

Already feeling better after changing, as I was rolling out my sleeping bag, a shuffle behind me made me jump. Glancing over my shoulder, Milton had removed his *Devil Horns* jacket and boots and was crawling inside with his own sleeping bag…and a pistol. Which only meant one thing. He was going to sleep in there with me.

Shimmying down into my sleeping bag, I watched as he rolled his out, eventually doing the same. Keeping a firm grip on the gun rested against his chest, he shut off the light and breathed out a long, deep breath.

There wasn't anything to say, and yet, it was like a million unspoken words floated between us. I knew nothing about the man next to me, which didn't make sense for me to feel this safe with him. Protected.

I knew he wouldn't unzip my sleeping bag and force himself in next to me. He wouldn't pull down my panties to have his wicked way with me just because we were alone. Hold me down and drive himself deep inside of me…

I swallowed hard, my body getting weirdly hot and insides tickly. What the hell was I *thinking*?

"You should sleep." The sound of his voice made my entire body jump. He knew I was still awake. Thank God he didn't know why. "No one will mess with us."

No, but I was thinking about you messing with me.

"Do you always sleep with a gun?"

He grunted. "Yes."

Does Blake know you're sharing a tent with me? I wanted to ask next but didn't because I already knew that answer. *No.*

"Where is Blake?" I couldn't help but ask, worried if he decided to appear out of nowhere.

"Passed out."

I nibbled my lower lip, not sure how to phrase my next question. "And he doesn't…"

"No, he doesn't." It surprised me that he understood what I meant to say, and my lungs deflated with relief that Blake didn't know where we were.

"Thank you," I say quietly, not sure if he heard me or not, but meaning every word.

He wouldn't find me tonight. Closing my eyes, I drifted to sleep quickly, happy to have a place to sleep that night. I woke the next morning well-rested, unable to remember the last time I slept that well, and knowing it was thanks to Milton.

As I glanced over to see if he was still sleeping, I sat up when I saw Milton was no longer next to me. Crawling out of my sleeping bag, I poked my head out of the tent. He was outside with Nicolas, talking about something I only caught the end of. "—to leave today. Jerome stood him up. I'm going ahead to clean up. You follow with the bitch."

"And what about the rest of them?" Milton asked, and Nicolas shook his head, neither of them noticing me yet.

"They'll stay for the whole weekend. I'm getting him out of here before some catch wind he's broken up."

Shoving his helmet on, Nicolas walked away. After he climbed on his bike and rode away, Milton turned in my direction, like he knew I was looking all along. My face flushed, and I tried to smooth down my wild curls as he said, "We're leaving."

We left not long after. Blake and Nick got back early to get rid of Grady's body, so the other members didn't see once they came back, and the girls had their lives threatened if they said a word.

No one did, and all was forgotten.

Saturday night rolled around quickly, and it was party on. The club filled up, and as always, I dressed up. Blake picked out a tight red number with a short skirt and low neckline to wear and had Florence do my makeup.

Blake nudges my arm. I'm sitting next to him at a table where a game of poker is going down. Blake has won every game so far, and there's an aura of anger staining the air. "Get me a drink," he orders.

Leaving his side, I saunter over to the bar, tired already, even though the night's only getting started.

"Johnny," I say to the man covered in piercings and tattoos. I used to be terrified of him, especially when he'd start angrily cussing in Spanish whenever he got pissed. Though, according to Florence, he's a lover, not a fighter. "Blake wants a drink. Make it a double."

Blake shouldn't be drinking with the pain medication he's on. He didn't ask for a double, but I'm hoping that slipping in extra will knock him out. Or kill him.

Just as the drink is placed on the bar, Nicole appears next to me. "A vodka and coke, Jon baby," she says, fully dilated eyes swinging my way. "What are you looking at?"

My insides seethe, but I don't rise to her taunts. I never can. But then something catches my eye—a sparkle of a diamond. Dropping my gaze, an engagement ring sits on her thin finger. "You... You're engaged?"

"Yes." She smiles. "To Nicolas."

Nicolas? He's the last person I thought would ever get married, and he *hates* Nicole. I don't understand. "Aren't you going to congratulate me?"

"Congratulations," I mumble and grab Blake's drink, taking it back to him. My heart pumps in my chest as I take my seat next to him, knowing she will never leave this place.

Blake turns to look at me, eyes lowering to my chest in a way that makes my stomach turn. "Come here." He pats his lap, and my insides bristle with unease, not wanting to do this right now. Standing, I go to sit on his lap, but he chuckles and stops me. "No. I meant on your knees."

Blake's men snicker as flames smack me in the face. "What?"

"You heard me. On your knees." He's never asked me to do anything like this before in front of everyone. "What the fuck are you waiting for?"

My bottom lip shakes as I lower myself to the ground, the floor sticky and damp beneath my knees, knowing everyone is now watching. "There you go, baby girl. Now suck me off."

"Blake...please—"

His nostrils flare, temper rising, which I know could be bad for me. It's been a week without him doing anything to me, and I can tell that the reprimand will be way worse.

"*Do it.*" I reach up with shaky hands to undo his belt, mortified and angry that he's making me do this right now. He continues his game, slamming a card on the table. I can't believe he's still playing poker while making me do this.

"The merch is someplace safe," the conversation that was happening between them resuming. "The feds will never find it." Blake nods, eyeing me with impatience as I undo his jeans, my heart thumping with sickness. Hatred. Hoping he will change his mind. "We're setting up profiles now—"

"No. Not online." I unzip him. "They know how to get into our sites." Jerking his hips upward, I peel back the layers. Jeans, boxers. "Shut them down."

"How do you—"

"The auction. That swanky place in Roseland." His cock, hard and angry, springs free, and a tear falls from my eye that he's making me do this with an audience.

His hand slams against the side of my head, sending a burst of stars firing across my vision. Without giving me a chance to recover from his assault, Blake fists my hair and yanks me forward. Sweat and salt choke me as he shoves himself into my mouth, past my teeth, until he's hitting the back of my throat. I'm gagging before I know it, the taste of him always vile. Always retched.

"We give them the goods, we get the money. Easy and undetectable," Blake continues as if I weren't on my knees being degraded. The club door opens and then slams shut. "Milton. You're back."

My heart leaps, and I try to pull away, but Blake keeps me in place, thrusting upward in a warning. My eyes water, lips stretched, and stomach rolling.

"Come play with us," Blake says. *No.* Please don't.

The chair next to us pulls out from beneath the table, and I sense him sit. Then I hear cards being shuffled. The other players have gotten quiet.

"That your blood?" Blake asks, voice heavy from me doing the only thing I can think of for this to end sooner. Making him come as quickly as I can. I've never felt shame like it, having no choice but to do what I can do.

"I'll live," Milton replies. "Is that necessary?"

"Why? You want my girl, Milton?" My insides twist, shock drawing me back. Blake bursts out laughing. "I'm just fucking with you." He grabs my hair and pulls me back. "Go to bed. You can finish later."

Getting to my feet, I keep my head down as I scurry out of the room, feeling a hundred pairs of eyes watching me go. Especially Milton's.

CHAPTER EIGHTEEN

I've always wondered what it would be like when you die. Where you go. If Heaven and Hell exist. That we're not all bullshitting ourselves in believing there are truly places for good and bad people. And what about the people in between? The ones who had no choice but to do wrong to survive. Do they stay here on earth, floating through it unseen? Unheard?

Then there's reincarnation, and maybe that would be nice. Be reborn a different person—someone with a better life unless you really are *that* unlucky to strike a lousy life twice.

Rain falls outside. Tap, tap, tapping on my window. They just administered my night meds, and already my eyes are heavy. My insides numb. There's a deep void in my chest, and it's called defeat.

"What are you thinking?" a voice drifts into my thoughts. How beautiful that voice is. How much I wish it could be real.

"I'm thinking…about where you go when you die," I mumble, eyes closing. "Anything would be better than this."

There's no reply. Not that I expect it from a ghost. A lone tear rolls over my nose and dampens my pillow before giving up and succumbing to the drugs.

SOMETHING WAKES ME. A BREATH THAT IS NOT MY OWN. A GUT instinct that I might not be truly alone. Over the years, I've learned that sensation well, mostly if Blake were in one of his evil moods and wanted to ruin something. Usually me.

As my eyes peel open, I warily search the room, expecting to see just another nurse or tech checking in on me. My breathing hitches when I see *him* instead. As clear as if it were fucking daytime, Milton's here, sat in the chair and piercing me with a frosty gaze.

Wearing a black suit and white shirt undone at the neck, his hair is perfectly in place, the murky shine in his eyes causing my stomach to shudder. And tingle. And clench.

"Hello, Heidi." His tone is silky smooth and yet deadly at the same time. Holding up his hand, he presents my journal. "This..." He opens it, flicking through the pages that are no longer blank since I decided to write the only thought I had inside my head. Him.

Milton Xavier Hood. Milton Xavier Hood.

Milton Xavier Hood. Milton Xavier Hood.

Slapping it closed, he throws it down on the table, the thud of the cover hitting the wood making me jump. "Is a little obsessive for someone you claim to hate so much, isn't it?"

He opens the folder next, eyes scanning the new notes on the pages. After reading, he closes that too, the crease between his brows intensifying. "Dr. Rogue claims to have had a breakthrough with you—"

"Milton," I interject, voice barely a whisper and disgustingly needy.

"Why have you been asking for me?"

The lump in my throat grows thicker, and my eyes burn. "Help me. Please."

His head tilts to the side. "Help you?"

Grabbing my blanket, I try to push it off me. As I lamely attempt to sit up, I groan, my head so dizzy. My hand slips beneath me, and I topple out of bed and crash to the floor, gasping from the pain as I land awkwardly on my neck.

He remains seated and doesn't make a move to help me as I grab his leg in another pitiful attempt, knowing how I must look as I pull myself up. Knowing how *weak* he must think I am. "I knew you were real. I knew. But they...they didn't believe me. They did this to me." Staring up at him, seeing the corners of his mouth lift into the sliest smirk I've ever seen him wear, the realization is the deadliest pill I've had to swallow so far.

"Did I not tell you you'd regret it?" His words puncture holes inside of me, splintering my heart. And it hurts. Oh, it fucking *hurts*.

He did this to me.

"It was you." My chest caves, his face so impassive it sets my nerves on fire with rage that seems to come from nowhere. He had them reduce me to *this*.

Exhaling through his nose, he leans forward. "You have five seconds to tell me why you want me here."

My eyes close with disgust, hating the moisture in my eyes. All for *him*. Sitting up and leaning against the bed frame, I lift my hands and clap them together. "Congratulations, Milton. What a performance. I suppose Nick was part of your brilliant plan as well? How long have you been planning this?"

"Nick?" He goes silent, lines creasing his forehead. *"Impossible,"* I think he says to himself before standing so quick the chair crashes to the floor behind me. "You're *lying*."

"Stop the act—"

"This *isn't* a fucking act!" Bending over, he picks me up off of the floor, a cry of surprise leaving my mouth as he slams my body down onto the bed. "Don't lie to me."

"I'm not, you are! He told me Blake is coming for me at Elise's wedding. He wants me back." He's silent for several moments, hands gripping my shoulders so tight I groan from the pressure.

He lets go. "Nicolas wasn't my doing."

Fisting the tears out of my eyes, I turn away, bottom lip trembling. Then I flinch when Milton's fingers lightly touch the bruises on my neck. Bruises everyone else ignored, thinking I did it myself. His touch is gone, and footsteps sound on the floor. I turn back, seeing he's already yanking the door open.

"Where are you going?" He doesn't stop. "Milton!"

Without looking at me, he leaves, slamming the door behind him. As I listen to his footsteps get further away, it slowly sinks in that he's not going to help me, and that once again, I have nobody.

CHAPTER NINETEEN

A week has passed, and Milton hasn't come back, but he stopped the cruel tricks. Because of my *good behavior*, they stopped giving me sedatives and started letting me out of my room. I've slowly gotten strength back into my legs, encouraged to exercise and eat, no longer weighed down by drug-induced lethargy. Though it's taken its toll.

After all, breaking down, picking yourself up, and trying again is exhausting when doing it for the hundredth time. It squeezes the life out of you as if something unknown is trying its hardest to stop you.

Are you sure you want to? Are you sure you don't want to die instead?

With my restrictions all lifted, Gabriella calls on Friday to tell them she's taking me out on Saturday for bridesmaid dress shopping. Elise wants to get married in June, and it's nearing December. The wedding will be here suddenly…and my time will be up.

Gabriella arrives early Saturday morning. Dressed in a conservative silk suit, her hair curled and makeup perfect, she looks vivacious. "I was on Haven FM this morning talking about my new book. Five-star reviews. You should be proud of me," she says while driving.

"*So* proud," I sarcastically reply, not knowing why I expected her to be concerned about why she hasn't been able to see me in a while. But I suppose it doesn't matter how many times you put a fresh coat of paint over something. If there's mold there to begin with, it will eventually seep through, and Gabriella is decaying behind the paint.

"Glad to see you're back to yourself. Sarcasm and all." I turn to look out of the window because anything is better than looking at her. Even at the city I hate. "What were all the theatrics about anyway? They said you attacked a nurse," she mocks. "I told them you wouldn't do such a thing."

"I nearly strangled her."

"Oh." She pauses. "Must've been the medication they were giving you. Probably disagreed. I'm beginning to question this facility. It seems they don't care about their staff or patients. Poor Ashley—the only decent doctor in the place is getting terrible treatment. And underpaid!" I stiffen at the mention of Dr. Rogue. I haven't seen her in days either. She canceled our appointment due to a family emergency, and a temp has taken her place in the clinic.

We eventually arrive at our destination. It's a little bridal boutique named Lenore's—everything that would make a single, loveless person's stomach churn. And mine does. Repeatedly.

Elise is waiting with her best friend, Olivia when we go inside. She's every bit as snooty, and privileged as you would expect the daughter of a judge to be, purposefully avoiding eye contact with me when we go over to them.

"Heidi." Elise's hands fall on my shoulder, and for a moment, it seems like she wants to pull me into a hug. Thankfully, she doesn't. "Thank you so much for agreeing to be my bridesmaid. It means a lot to me."

I should tell her that I didn't agree to anything and was forced to keep her happy, but I don't. Maybe because I feel slightly sorry for what she's marrying. "Do you have any idea of what colors you want your bridesmaids to wear?" Gabriella interrupts, browsing dresses on a rack, her nose turning up at a few of them.

"I was thinking pink or gray," she replies. "What do you think, Olivia?"

"Any would go well with the white roses you chose. And lovely for summertime."

Slumping in one of the plush antique chairs, I listen as they continue discussing dress colors and styles. Bored out of my mind already, my thoughts a million miles away, a woman appears from behind a white floor-length curtain and wanders over to us.

Lenore, I'm guessing, given how *well-to-do* she looks.

"Lowdon, I presume?" she asks with a smile that screams, *give me your money!*

Eyeing me sagged in the chair, confusion wriggles her brow, and I'm pretty sure she's wondering if I've wandered in from the street for a place to sit. I'm wearing Elise's old clothes again. My pale and gaunt face adds to the hobo look, my hair scraped back into a scruffy knot. When she notices I've caught her in her staring act, she quickly averts her gaze, cheeks turning red. "Which one of you is the bride?"

"That would be me." Elise steps forward, holding out her hand to shake Lenore's. "It's lovely to meet you, Lenore. My stepmother here tells me you're the best in the city, and I have been admiring your dresses for years."

Lenore turns to Gabriella, a grateful smile spreading over her lips. "Why, thank you. It's a pleasure to meet you all." *Except me.* "Now, Elise, would you like to go first or your bridesmaids?"

"Bridesmaids, please. I can browse while they change. I'm not quite sure what I want."

"Of course."

"This is my maid of honor, Olivia, and my little sister, Heidi," she introduces us, and for some reason, it makes me think of Nicole. My real sister, who Gabriella insists doesn't exist, wondering if she's gotten married to Nicolas yet. He didn't mention while he was threatening me. Though, I know love isn't what put that cheap diamond ring on her finger. It's just a front to hide the lies.

"Let's get started. I couldn't help overhearing you mention a few of the colors that are, in fact, in this season's collection. I will take your measurements first, Olivia, and then Heidi next before we look at some dresses."

Lenore takes Olivia away. After she finishes, she and Elise look at dresses while Gabriella stays with me. Though, I have sneaky a suspicion she's guarding. "Smile, would you?" she says through her teeth as Lenore makes her way over to us. "You look miserable."

"You're next, Heidi," Lenore says, taking my measurements with a white tape. "I think an off the shoulder gown would suit them both. Especially Heidi, such a delicate frame, and a popular choice."

"Yes, I agree," Gabriella nods, though I wonder how she really feels about me getting a compliment.

After choosing a few dresses for us to try on, I follow Lenore into the changing rooms. "Are you sure you don't want help?"

"I'm sure." The last thing I want is someone like her seeing the scars tarnishing parts of my skin. After she leaves, I lock the door.

Knowing there's no way to get out of this, I start undressing and grab the first dress on the rail; an off-the-shoulder pale rose one. After putting it on and zipping the side, I slip on the heels Lenore provided and sigh as I observe myself in the mirror.

"You look beautiful, baby girl," Blake says behind me, large arms encircling my waist. Ice-cold eyes slide up and down my reflection and makes me instantly sick. "Fuckable."

He kisses my neck, and I bow my head, tearing my eyes away from the sickening sight of us in the mirror. He grabs my throat viciously, forcing me to look back into the mirror. "Stop Blake—"

"Look at yourself, baby girl." His tongue glides up the side of my throat, his eyes locked with mine on the mirror's surface. "This body of yours could kill a man." He pushes me forward, slamming me into the glass. As he presses into me, I weep. "And you do kill me. You kill me and send me to heaven every time I slip right into your tight cunt." He yanks up my dress. "Watch me go to heaven, baby." He jerks my panties to the side, the fabric cutting into my hips. "Watch me die."

A light knock on the door snaps me from my thoughts. I breathe out, realizing my entire body is shaking.

"I'm...I'm not ready," I shout, thinking it's Lenore come to check on me. There's no reply, and when I glance over my shoulder, a chill rushes down my spine, despite knowing it can't possibly be anyone other than one of the girls. Knowing I'm being silly, I walk over to the door and twist the lock. "I said I'm not—" My mouth drops. "Milton?"

Clashing with the pearl décor wearing all black, Milton stands before me. He steps forward, and I stumble back, my heart racing as he closes the door behind him and locks it. "You can't be in here."

"Nice dress."

"You do realize Gabriella and Elise are just outside. You need to leave before they know I'm in here with you."

"There was a break-in," he reveals, leaning his back against the wall, his hair slightly mussed from the wind outside

"What?"

"Nicolas. Someone smuggled him in during visiting hours, and your door was left unlocked that night after I'd left clear instructions for it to be locked. When he was done with you, he got out without detection, so you know what that means?"

I swallow hard. *Shit.* "He has someone on the inside."

"Yes, which complicates things for me." Because the whole building heard me shout his name, and if it's true that Nick has someone on the inside at Stonehill, he knows Milton is alive.

"What are you going to do?" I ask.

Leaning off the wall, he slowly walks around me, eyes scanning the length of the dress I'm wearing. "Why did you ask me for help?"

There's a knock and the doorknob rattles. I gasp, but it seems Milton locked the door after him. "How's it going in there, Heidi?" It's Elise.

"Answer her," Milton mouths, not moving.

"F-fine!" I call out. "Sorry, I'm still changing."

"That's okay. Olivia hates the pink one." She sighs. "What do you think?"

The side of Milton's lip curls upward ever so slightly. *He likes it.* With that, a different kind of pleasure tingles the base of my spine. Would that mean...No. It couldn't be. There's no way he's attracted to me. "I hate it."

His smile widens. "Okay, well, skip to the next dress, and I will see you out there."

After she walks away, Milton chortles. "Look at you, bonding with your stepsister."

"You need to go. We can't do this now."

"Answer my question. Why did you ask for my help?" he demands, and when I say nothing, he steps forward. My back smacks into the mirror behind me as he demands, "*Tell* me."

"Because..." My shoulders slump, hating that he's making me say it. "You're the only one I've ever felt safe with."

His eyebrow lifts. "And yet, you fucked me over."

"I will sign your stupid contract, okay? Do whatever the hell you want. I can't go back there...I—" A lump lodges in the back of my throat. "For God's sake. Do you want me to beg you?"

"I hope you understand what you're asking." His fingers catch the material of the dress, and he tugs me forward. I inhale sharply as I slam into him. Capturing my chin, he forces me to look at him. "Because once you sign..." His thumb rubs against my bottom lip, and for one paralyzing moment, I think he's going to kiss me. And the thought of that is enough to stop my heart. "You're fucking mine."

The word confuses me. Shocks me. Mine. *His.*

The paths laid out in front of me have their own twists and bends. Go back to the club to be Blake's bitch and have him put a baby back in me. Be forced to end it—open my veins and bleed. But then, they win, and I lose.

Then there's Milton. Whoever he is now, whatever he is a part of, is a mystery I'd be walking blind into. I could be stepping into something I might not ever get out of, where he might decide he's not finished punishing me.

With my heart in my throat, I nod, because what choice do I have? He lets go. "Fine."

"Fine," I echo, voice quivering as he turns and leaves. Slamming my head back against the glass, I breathe out heavily. What the fuck have I done?

CHAPTER TWENTY

After Gabriella signs me back in and I return to my room, I don't know what to do with myself. Milton didn't tell me when his *help* would begin. As I pace my room, my body on edge, the nurses call us to the cafeteria for dinner. I'm not hungry, but I line up with the rest of the zombie girls. When the line dwindles, I'm about to grab an apple from the stand when a scream pierces my ears.

"Don't touch me!" Looking over my shoulder, a girl around my age kicks a male temp trying to calm her in the balls. "I'm a saint! I would *never* put it in my mouth!"

Some girls laugh, those I would genuinely call crazy, as nurses and orderlies surround the dark-haired girl, quickly escorting her out. Something she only laughs at.

Abandoning the apple, I return to my room. Back to pacing back and forth. Back. Forth. Forth. Back.

It could be another week before I see Milton again. He could keep me in here, tormenting me with fear as further punishment. At this point, after what he did during the past few weeks, I wouldn't put it past him. And I marvel at how I *still* begged for his help after he reduced me to nothing but a drooling lemming. How desperate can I be?

Vera suddenly enters my room, face blank of emotion. "You. Let's go."

"Go?" I echo, but she's already turning and walking out. Running to catch her, we go down the corridor and end up at the doors which lead to Milton's office. The side of the building that's been closed for fifteen years.

It takes everything inside of me not to look smug as I cross my arms. "Where am I *going* Vera?" I ask irately when she stops by the doors and opens one of them.

Sighing tiredly, she avoids eye contact. "Just go."

Glaring at her with disgust, I shove past her and continue alone. Down the long, eerie corridor to the other side of the building I knew all along was there. Once reaching the end, I hesitate before pushing open the door.

Déjà-fucking-vu.

Everything appears the same, the last rays of daylight streaming through the large windows, creating a haze of welcome and warmth—what a lie.

Someone approaches me from behind. "Hello, Miss Adams," Lisa says, a weird friendly smile in place, considering the last time we were in each other's company, I'd been somewhat threatening. "If you would follow me. We don't have a lot of time."

"Where's Milton?" I wonder.

"Attending to a last-minute matter." Taking me into the office, she retrieves two black boxes from a cabinet; one bigger than the other and tied together with a blood-red ribbon. Placing them down on the desk, she hands me an envelope before leaving and shutting the door.

My scalp prickles. Annoyed by the secrecy, I rip it open and pull out a piece of white card.

If you want to be part of my world, then you must look the part. — M

Dropping the note, I untie the ribbon and slip the lid off the larger box first. Pulling back the white tissue inside reveals neatly folded black fabric. Lifting it by its straps, I take a small step back as the skirt billows to the floor, revealing a V-neck floor-length chiffon gown.

My lips part in shock and awe, having never seen a dress like it in my life. It's beautiful and elegant, and now I'm nervous. Because I know a pretty garment like this one would be worn to visit the devil. Inside the next box is a pair of black heels, a sprinkle of diamonds along the strap to go with the dress.

If you want to be part of my world, then you must look the part.

Inhaling a deep breath, I strip my clothes and slip into the gown. As I pull the straps up over my shoulders, I'm surprised by how well it fits. I can't help admiring the daring slit at the midthigh of the flowy skirt after putting on the shoes. It's a shame that it's like dressing a second-hand doll in a new outfit. I'm every bit a knockoff.

A thump on the door signals Lisa's return, and when she enters, the smile is still intact. "Did the dress and shoes fit to your liking?" All I can do is nod. "Very good. You will be meeting with Mr. Hood in a little while. We have a stop to make beforehand."

Again. So secretive.

We go back into the private lot, and a car with a driver is waiting for us. My teeth chatter, the wintery breeze biting as I climb into the back of the car as Lisa gets in the other side.

Once the car begins moving, she presents another box, this one significantly smaller. "Milton *insists* you put this on."

I've seen the box before, knowing the X ring resides inside. My new shackle. Maybe putting it on is some sort of test that makes everything final. Sighing deeply, I open the box, and there it sits, shiny and unsightly. "He really loves his rings."

I slip it on my index finger. A perfect fucking fit.

THE CAR STOPS IN FRONT OF A BEAUTY SALON. I THINK IT'S A JOKE at first, and I almost laugh. Unhinged Heidi gets to be Cinderella for a day. Following Lisa inside, the salon is spacious—gleaming white floors and walls. "Why am I here?" I question, conscious of the eyes watching me.

Ignoring my question, Lisa steps forward to address a young woman behind the counter. "Hi, can I help you?" she asks brightly.

"An appointment with Bethany."

"She's with a client at the moment—"

"Then I insist you interrupt," she interjects, the request sounding more urgent with her accent.

Picking up the phone, she mumbled a few rushed words in it, cheeks flushed red. "Terribly sorry. She's on her way," she says when she hangs up.

Seconds later, a woman bursts through a set of doors. "Lisa. My apologies for having kept you waiting." If this woman is Bethany, then she reminds me of a funky grandma. She's older, in her fifties maybe, with short white hair, the tips colored pink. Light blue eyes rimmed with pink eyeshadow flutter in my direction, shaped eyebrows rising with surprise. "Oh my…this one isn't like his usual."

"Bethany," Lisa sighs.

Walking forward, she takes my hand in hers. The directness makes me instantly uncomfortable. "Can I simply not compliment a woman? You are beautiful. What's your name?"

"Heidi," I answer before Lisa can get a word in. She seethes behind me.

"You *weren't* supposed to say your name. Milton—"

"Lisa, relax," Bethany cuts her off, putting her arm around my shoulder. "Go sit down and put your feet up. I will send Carly over with a mimosa." She turns back to me. "Now come with me. I promise you will blow his mind once I'm done with you."

Blow Milton's mind? I can't help the snort, and she glances at me questioningly. "It's not like that."

"*Riiight*," she winks, not believing me. Keeping hold of my hand, we enter a different room. Sitting me in the chair, she gets to work right away, twisting my hair up into pin curlers in silence. She works like this for a while until I can't help the question burning my tongue. "What did you mean about me not being his usual?"

"You caught that, huh?" she says, giggling a little. "Well, for starters, I've never been sent a blond before by that man. And an absolutely stunning one at that. Not to say the others weren't pretty—but they were *pretty plain* if you ask me. Quiet. Timid.

Not a word out of them. And I mean not a single word. It was like trying to squeeze water out of a melon."

Her openness pushes me to ask the next question, "And there were a lot of them?"

"When Milton was younger, one a week." My eyes widen. That many? "Lately, however, no. Few and far between. You've been his first in I don't know how long…Maybe the last?"

I sigh. "If by that you mean pissing him off until he's put off women forever, then yes, I will be the last. Trust me, I'm a massive inconvenience."

"Are you sure about that?" she questions, raising her eyebrow again. And I can't answer, because I'm not sure about it myself. "I can definitely see the allure. I was quite taken aback when Lisa walked through the door with you. You know, I'm not supposed to say this, but we all wondered what exactly he did with all those women."

My fingers mess with the fabric on my dress as I ask, "Did you ever find out?"

After securing the last pin, she moves around the chair until she's facing me. Picking up cream, she dabs it on my face and feels nice when she rubs it in. "No…though there are plenty of rumors circulating about that mansion of his. The one he owns with Mr. Koslov. Not sure if you've ever seen him. I've only caught glimpses myself. Terrifyingly handsome, and like Milton, an absolute enigma. Apparently, best friends. Anyhow, rumor has it, Milton runs a sex cult there."

"A *sex cult?*"

Bethany smiles as she starts applying the foundation to my face. "I know. Sounds rather out there, doesn't it? But yes, that is the rumor mill. I mean, there's certainly more to Milton that meets the eye." She blends in my foundation with a damp sponge. "Who knows? Maybe he's into that kind of kink? I know Mr. Koslov *has* to be. Men that beautiful can't be vanilla." She sighs wistfully, eyes clouded in thought, almost as if she wouldn't mind knowing if it's the truth or not. She then laughs when she catches me staring, flabbergasted by all this maybe fake information she's dumped on my lap. "Listen to me, letting my mouth run away with me. I better shut up before Lisa hears me talking about her *master*. Lord knows, she'll rip me apart."

A little while later, after taking the pins from my hair and putting down one of the many makeup brushes, she stands back to admire her work. "Whether you think that man likes you or not, he will now."

Turning, I glance at myself in the mirror. The creature that stares back resembles me but isn't. She's beautiful, her blond hair no longer dull and flat. It's shiny, curled, and longer than it's ever been. Makeup compliments her dress, eyes dusted in kohl to make them pop, offset by a nude lip.

"He won't resist." My stomach flutters at her words. I want to tell her again; it's not like that, but my mouth won't cooperate.

Because it *is* like that. It always has been.

CHAPTER TWENTY-ONE

The building we pull up to is nothing like I've ever seen before—the kind of place only the elite of Fair Haven frequent, reeking of class and wealth. Even elegantly wrapped and primped, I don't exude such things. I look the part, but beneath this creature's skin, I'm still me—a damn mess.

Milton is waiting in the foyer as I enter alone. A multitude of different sensations washes through me when I see him. A prickle of hate. A shot of unease. A dose of attraction.

There's no way to deny how exceptionally handsome he looks tonight. Dressed impeccably in a charcoal three-piece suit, I'm rendered speechless. He hasn't noticed me yet, and the closer I get, the more the heat sears my skin. For the first time tonight, I'm toasty warm when I shouldn't be anything but icy cold.

Catching his eye, my stomach tumbles as his gaze instantly lowers. It's not apparent as to what he thinks as he takes in my appearance. Probably thinking what a fake I am. Nerves squeeze the life out of my chest as he reaches for my hand, his thumb rubbing against the metal of the ring once I'm in his grasp. I'm not sure why the meager thought of him being happy I'm wearing it pleases me, but it does.

Placing my hand into the crook of his arm, the smell of him makes my insides ache as he leads me into the restaurant. He smells good—of rich cologne and something familiarly *him*. We draw attention from men and women waiting in the foyer, and I swear I'm not imagining Milton's grip tightening on me. I don't *want* to imagine it.

Making our way over to a hostess standing behind a mahogany podium, she politely nods even though pink colors her cheeks in Milton's presence. "We have your table ready, sir. This way." Again, he says nothing, and I wonder what's wrong with him as she walks ahead. He's never usually so quiet. Reserved.

Following the woman past the bustling restaurant where other people are dining, we enter one of the private rooms with a table set for two. It's intimate, but not constricting, and noticeably quieter. Soft music trickles in through speakers as Milton pulls out my chair for me.

I sit, muscles tense as he circles the table and sits opposite. The hostess leaves, and a male waiter donning a smart black suit replaces her. "Good evening to you both. My name is Harry, and I will be looking after you this evening. May I start you off with drinks? A glass of wine, perhaps?"

"Sure," Milton finally speaks, fingers drumming on the table. *Drum, drum, drum.* "A bottle of Cheval Blanc."

"Excellent choice, sir," Harry says with a bow of the head before leaving. I spot water on the table and reach to grab it, not able to recall the last time I drank something.

"I took the liberty of ordering for you," Milton says when my mouth is full of water. "If we're going to do this, you will eat properly."

I swallow in one painful gulp when the waiter reappears, presenting a deep red bottle. With Milton's nod of approval, he pours wine into our glasses, finishing with a practiced twist of the wrist to avoid marring the pure, white table linen.

Once filled, I reach for my glass and take a mouthful of that too, sensing I'm in for one hell of a night. "You're uncomfortable here," Milton observes once the waiter is out of earshot. "And...*twitchy*."

Sighing, I place my elbows on the table and take them off again, remembering somewhere deep in my psyche that it's not the proper etiquette for a fancy place like this. *Thank you, Gabriella.* "You know I'm not used to this."

"You can relax." He waves his hand. "It's not like I'm going to strangle you before the starter has even arrived—"

"I'm not sleeping with you," I blurt, watching his right eyebrow rise, an action I'm beginning to think he does whenever I surprise him. But I can't help it, my earlier conversation with Bethany playing on my mind.

"Who said anything about *that*?" he questions, but I'm saved from answering with Harry's return.

"Your starters," he announces, placing small dishes in front of us, much to Milton's aggravation with the disruption. "Hand dived scallops with truffle vinaigrette. Enjoy."

Instead of picking up his starter fork, he suddenly grabs my leg from under the table and tugs me forward. "What are—"

Angling his body to the side, he props my foot on his lap to fix the strap that has come undone on my shoe. For a moment, I'm at a loss for words, the heat from his hand doing terrible things to my insides.

"You think I want to fuck you?" he asks, so cutthroat, it takes me a while to answer.

"I don't know *what* you want." I breathe out, his skin on mine sending spasms of electricity up my leg. "Just because I've handed myself over to you doesn't mean I'm a sex toy for your enjoyment."

"A sex toy?" His shoulders shake with silent laughter, and I flush. "Well, I don't know where this has come from…but there's one massive difference here." Wrapping his fingers around my ankle, he pulls me forward until my back lifts off the chair. Capturing me around the waist, he drags me onto his lap, using the slit in my dress to his advantage to reach inside and grab my thighs.

I moan before realizing. From his touch. The closeness. God, I hate myself. What the fuck is wrong with me? His breath brushes against my face. My lips. "I don't think you've ever wanted anything as bad."

His large hands caress upward, catching my hips beneath the dress in a firm grip. He jerks me forward then, his thigh causing friction against my core. The ache comes back with a vengeance as he does it again. And again. Until he has me slowly dry humping him in a restaurant and whimpering for him like he's crack.

"Milton…" I squeeze the lapel of his jacket, needing him to stop. Not wanting him to stop.

"You're right." Eyes flash with amusement as he suddenly lifts me and puts me back on the chair. The loss of contact makes my body slump in gut-wrenching disappointment. "You're not here for that." Reaching inside his inner pocket, he pulls out a piece of paper and pen. "You aren't eating."

"I've lost my appetite," my voice quivers as he pushes the paper and pen toward me.

"Sign it." My hand trembles as I pick up the pen, a jumble of complicated words peering back at me. My hesitation makes him sigh. "You either want my help, or you don't. It's not like I wanted to consider this—"

Scribbling my name along the dotted line, I throw the pen down on the table dramatically. "Then, why did you? You could have told me no. Told *me* to go to hell. So why?"

"*Logic*," he bites back icily, like the tension that happened between us only moments ago didn't. "Blake has something I want, and now I have something he wants. There's really nothing more to it."

"Blackmail?" I dryly reply, and he shrugs offhandedly. "Then I guess it's a *pleasure* doing business with you."

"Pleasure's all mine," he grits out through his teeth, and I can't bear the pain in my heart that he can be so callous. So fucking cruel and unaffected. But what did I expect?

Smothering back tears, I change the subject, "Am I to keep staying at Stonehill?"

He picks up his glass and takes a sip. "I can't trust Nicolas will stay away from, so no, I'm moving you someplace else."

Moving me. Like I'm nothing more than an undesired object to be picked up and placed wherever. "What about Gabriella? Dr. Rogue?"

He avoids eye contact now. "Nothing to worry yourself with."

"I'll need to know what to say to Gabriella when I have to do bridesmaid duties. And what about the wedding itself—"

His eyes snap up, stopping me sharp. "What do you think is happening here?"

"What do you mean?"

"Fuck *sake*, Heidi," he sneers with frustration. "Must I spell it out to you? You won't *be* at the wedding. You can't be spotted outside. In fact, I believe you staying in Fair Haven—"

"I'm *leaving*?" My insides clench. "With you?"

Picking up his fork, he stabs a scallop and puts it in his mouth. He chews and chews and then swallows. "No," he replies, woodenly. It doesn't appear as though he has much of an appetite either. "Not with me. On your own."

My heart sinks. "What about…us?"

"Us? There *is* no us." *Ouch.* "Fortunately for you, I take what that ring on your finger means seriously. You're protected whether I like it or not." Lines of torment crease his face, an emotion I can't name crossing over his eyes, making them shadowy. "When I'm around you…all I want is to hurt you."

It takes everything to keep my composure as our conversation dies. The waiter reappears to take our dishes away, and when he comes back moments later, he's putting another meal in front of us. "Roast chicken breast with potato puree and pine nuts. Would you like a refill, Miss?"

After nodding, he tops up my glass and leaves. I take a drink, already feeling the effect of the wine fuzzing my edges. This time, I do pick up my dinner fork. Whether to keep from going insane or because I'm hungry, I don't know. The food is delicious, and I eat every bit, knowing it could be my last meal with a person if Milton's new plan for me comes to fruition.

Slowly, it dawns on me the true extent of what signing my name on that bit of paper meant. I'm about to lead a long, lonely existence just like the man sitting opposite of me, and maybe that's my true punishment for what I did to him. Like I haven't endured enough.

"The place you took me to the other week...Club X, Lisa called it. What do you do there?"

His fingers are back to drumming on the table. "Why?"

"Just curious. Those other women—you brought them there, right? Why did it never work with them?"

Dropping his fork, he wipes his mouth with a napkin. "I see you and Bethany had an interesting conversation."

"Maybe." I mess with the tablecloth. "She thinks you run a sex cult."

A muscle jumps in his neck. "Does she now?"

"Can I see?"

"No, and out of perplexed curiosity, why the fuck would you have the slightest interest if it were the truth?"

"I've just found out that I'm about to spend the rest of my goddamn days as your prisoner, Milton," I say, body shaking with anger and hurt, and God knows what else this psycho has done to me. "The least you can do is answer my questions. Show me what *this* means." Holding up my hand, the ring sparkles in the candlelight. "Let's pretend that tonight, I'm not me. I'm just a woman you dressed up and made pretty at the salon. One you wined and dined—"

The ring of his phone cuts me off. His eyes spark with annoyance when he takes it out of his pocket and peers down at the screen. "This better be good," he bites into the phone and then hangs up seconds later. "Looks like you're about to get your fucking wish," he mumbles, standing up. "Let's go."

THERE ARE TWO REASONS WHY I KNOW WHERE WE'RE GOING EVEN before we leave Fair Haven. Milton's mood and the ball of dread in the depths of my stomach. We speed down the highway, and my knuckles turn white as I grip the seat. The journey is all too familiar as we turn off in the direction of the elusive Club X.

We go down the dirt road with thick trees and onward to the mansion. Resembling every bit like a conjured-up nightmare, I'm not entirely sure why I argued to see it again. I'm shaking as we pull into the driveway, mine and Milton's conversation weighing heavily on my mind.

Like last time, a man comes to take the car away after we get out. Grabbing my hand, a habit he seems to prefer, Milton takes me inside the creepy cold entranceway. He doesn't pause, pace quickening as he takes a right turn, letting go of me briefly to pull the key card from his pocket.

"Lucius," he addresses an older gentleman with dark eyes, a balding head, and wearing a tailored suit. "I'm taking you found what I was looking for?"

"Yes. He's in room eight. Anything else, sir?"

"No, that will be all." With a nod, the man leaves, and Milton pulls me in the opposite direction, the stairs that lead to the red tunnels.

Once underground, he lets go, and I trail after him as he storms ahead until we reach door eight, though there's no number visible on its paint. Throwing it open without pause, Milton steps inside and stops. "Why am I not surprised to see your face?"

Peeking around Milton's body, a man who appears to be in his twenties, stands from the seat he's sitting in. It's a bare room with only a table and one chair. Odd, given the big mystery surrounding these rooms. "Whatever you think I've done isn't true. Tell your boy he picked up the wrong guy."

"He's never wrong, and unlike you, someone I *trust*," he replies smoothly, calmly, but his clenched fists ruin the barely contained rage I know he's bottling inside. "What was it you were offered to betray me?"

The man shakes his head. "Betray you? I don't know what you're talking about."

"What was the offer you couldn't refuse Nicolas Santos to get to her?" I blink in shock when Milton points in my direction. This is the guy Nicolas used to get into Stonehill? "I'm waiting."

The man glances at me, but Milton steps to the side, blocking his view. "I don't know a Nicolas Santos," I hear him say, "I've never laid eyes on the bitch in my life."

"Don't lie to me. What *was* it?"

"Nothing, I swear."

Milton's body stiffens even more. "You were the only one working that night, so I will ask you again, what was it?" When there's silence, Milton takes a step forward to grab him, but the man stumbles back, and now I can see him—a face full of fear.

"No—wait! It's not what it looks like, it's just, I'm trying, okay? I *need* it."

"Need what? Fucking meth, is it?" Breathing out a heavy breath through his nose, I can only imagine Milton's expression as he says, "You betrayed me for meth?" He pulls out a gun from his jacket. *"Pity."*

Realizing his fate as Milton pulls back the trigger, the man's splutters, "W-Wait! I have kids!"

"They're better off." He pulls the trigger, and the gun fires. My legs stumble back, the chicken I ate churning in my stomach when I hear the distinctive *thud* as the man drops to the floor. My heart rams against my chest as I lean against the wall away from room eight, not sure why a man who hates me keeps killing for me.

CHAPTER TWENTY-TWO

Gazing into the fire, at the flames cavorting within the fireplace, it's so quiet you could hear a pin drop on the marble stone floor. Opposite, with a glass of spirit in hand, Milton sits with eyes clouded in thought. Ominous eyes. *Haunted.* We've been like this for a while. Both staring at the flames, I'm sure warms neither of us. My body shivers from witnessing him kill yet again—this one I'm not entirely sure deserved.

We're all addicts, in one way or another. We all crave. *Need.* It may not be the obvious kind of addiction, but it's still one.

"You have a question." My body jerks at the sound of his voice, his tone like a double-edged sword. *"Ask."*

Swallowing hard, the burn between my thighs comes back to taunt me. Why, I don't know. *Sick, sick, sick.* "What did that man do?"

"Tampered with surveillance," he answers tonelessly. "Hence why there wasn't an alert of a trespasser on my property. That man was part of my security team at Stonehill."

"You own Stonehill?"

"*Yes.* But you knew that already." My head lowers. He's right, but it was only an inkling. How else was he able to get around so quickly? "Is that all that man did?"

Eyes narrow. "Meaning?"

"You killed again for me."

"No. He was disloyal." My eyes flicker to his, and I shudder beneath his stern gaze. Reaching inside his pocket, he tosses the gun on the table between us. "This bothers you?"

Does it? Yes. No. I'm so confused. "What about his kids?"

His eyelids lower, lips pulling together. "They will be fine. And now I have a question for you." He takes a sip of his drink. "Do you still want to know what I do here, given what you've seen so far?"

"Yes." I don't lie, wanting to know more now than ever. I have to know his world. Whether that's just an excuse, I'm not sure. Could be. *Probably.*

The thought of him moving me away from him and Fair Haven in the name of protection doesn't sit well with me when all his secrets lie within these walls. And I might only have tonight to find out. "Ignorance is bliss, you know?"

My head shakes. "Stop trying to get out of it."

"Fine." Standing, he takes one step toward me. "I suppose I could humor your curiosity for the evening. First, though, I must see someone."

MILTON: WORSHIP

We head back out into the cold hall with the three arches. The silver X's displayed are like deadly weapons—rules to follow, or *else*. Milton takes me straight across, through a door that leads to a spacious room with a crowd of well-dressed people. Men in dark suits and women in beautiful evening dresses. It's like we've entered another world entirely.

If I didn't look hard enough between the cracks, I would have thought I'd entered one of Lawrence's parties on a Saturday night. Entertaining the type of people that flaunt their ugly personalities because they have all those pretty pennies to protect them.

This party is nothing like those ones. These people are different, like they'd use their money to do *more* than protect them.

Girls weave between the crowd, wearing scraps of material that's considered lingerie. They carry trays of drinks and smile as they serve. As we pass an L-shaped stage that divides the room of black leather seats and circular tables, my lips immediately part at the *show*.

Bent over and spread wide, a man rams a woman from behind, using her hair as his own personal leash as their naked skins slap together. It's a violent, brutal display with no pause to catch breaths. With her skin flushed and sweaty, instead of screaming at the man to stop, she yells, "More. *Harder!*"

The crowd murmurs their approval as they subtly watch, a sport for their enjoyment, soaking in all this sadism with greedy eyes. Meanwhile, here I am, just as bad as them. Throbbing inside. Unable to take my eyes off them. Stepping closer to Milton when a crowd of men pushes past me to get a closer look, I cling onto his arm, and that's when I notice he's been watching me all this time.

Glancing up to meet his gaze, some of his hair has fallen across his forehead. He doesn't move it away, and it makes him look dangerous. Sexy. And then I can't stop thinking about what it would be like to be bent over by him.

Thoughts like that will send a girl to Hell. Then again, I think I'm already here.

Taking my hand, Milton crosses the room to a large booth where a man sits with a girl on his knee and his hand down her panties—

"You're early tonight," Milton interrupts, stopping beside the table. The man removes his hand and leans back against the seat as the girl slumps with...relief?

"I'm *angry* tonight," he replies, a smile that looks both cruel and devilish at the same time, which contradicts his blond hair, tanned skin, and angelic features. No. There's nothing angel-like about this man. While he may be blessed by the heavens, he's granite, his appearance merely a mask. Power drips off every inch of his large frame—something that feels out of control. Volatile. Which I'm sure the girl feels too as she sits with a silver chain wrapped around her slim neck.

She's pretty, with dark hair and round eyes. Beneath them sit shadows of exhaustion. God knows what this man has done to her, though she isn't a victim. She's something else...something I can't quite grasp—

"I can see that," Milton stops my thoughts, head inclining toward the girl. "I gather your friend is aware of our policy?"

The man's fingers twist through the chain, making it tighter for her. She doesn't protest. "Of course. What about yours?"

Milton gives a quick glance over his shoulder, and I avoid his gaze. "Yes, she knows, alright." *She signed, alright.* He faces the man again while twisting his ring around his finger. "I'll leave you to your fun. I would say try not to make too much of a mess, but I beat you to it already."

Without saying goodbye, Milton guides me back toward the stage where the couple is still fucking. Beside me, Milton chuckles. "You look appalled."

"Why wouldn't I be?" I glare at him for making fun of me. He glances at the stage, amusement shining in his eyes as he looks at the scene. Seeing him watching makes my lower stomach clench.

Does *he* like it?

"These are Maxim's rooms, and your reaction has only shown me how unable you are to take on this role you've created for yourself."

"You said you would humor me. So far, all you've done is avoid."

He smiles, the moans of the couple in the background heating the skin on my face. Being this close to him is all too much, but I don't want to back down. "I was saying hello to my friend. And maybe I've changed my mind."

My eyes narrow. Why won't he show me? "I'll find them *myself.*" My declaration even surprises me. That I dare do it. Yet, he surprises me when a smile stretches his lips.

"Go ahead." He thrusts a card into my hand, and glancing down, the X key ridicules me. "Go pick a door."

"I will." With my stomach doing loops, I twist on my heel and head back to the foyer, taking the corridor to his side of the building.

Milton follows silently behind, eventually saying, "This side of you is quite entertaining to watch."

I don't reply as I unlock the doors and head for the tunnels. Once going down the steps, I stop at the bottom to eye the rows of black doors bleached red.

Which one to pick. I don't know. Certainly not room eight.

Milton comes up behind me, and my skin prickles with goosebumps when his fingers snake around my waist. "Go ahead. Pick one. But don't say I didn't warn you."

CHAPTER TWENTY-THREE

The ebony gloss faintly trimmed in red chrome shines on the door I've chosen. A detail I wouldn't have noticed unless I was this close. "This one," I say, my spine tingling when Milton reaches forward to push it open.

Behind door number one...

It takes a while for my sight to adjust from the glare in the corridor. At first, only darkness greets us until there's the faintest glow of candles against a wall.

He touches my shoulder, and I flinch, not entirely sure I *want* to do this anymore. Why do I want to put myself through this?

We all wonder what he does with all those women.

"You ready?" His breath is warm against my skin and makes the hairs on my neck stand on high alert. He's enjoying this—I know it. Taking his time, lapping up my reaction. *You've seen nothing yet, Heidi.* I don't doubt it. He knows there's trepidation dripping off me, and it's enough to steel my spine.

"Let's go." I walk inside bravely. *Too* brave. Stumbling in my heels, a gasp claws up my throat as I take in the scene before me. Either my eyes are the most deceitful, and I'm choo-chooing on the crazy train, or I am genuinely witnessing this.

The room is circular, the walls and ceiling made of stone and covered with hundreds of black candles. Their warm glow reflects off five evenly spaced columns bathed in red light. To each column a naked woman, donning a black mask to hide her identity, stands with hands cuffed above her head. And they're not alone.

Dark hooded figures stand before them. Assuming by their height and build, they're male. As my eyes squint to figure out what is actually happening, I'm shocked when I realize they're all engaging in sex.

Moans of pleasure from this sordid scene have me taking a step back, and my heart swoops in my chest when I bump into Milton's front. He's right behind me, watching me. Shit. Fuck. "Get undressed," he orders.

I whirl around to face him. "W-What?"

He laughs airily, though there isn't anything humorous about it. Nothing at all. My cheeks bristle with heat as he asks, "You wanted this, did you not?"

Clutching my dress, I move away from him, head shaking. His jaw clenches, and with just one step, closes in on me.

I whelp as he catches my skirt and wrenches me forward. "Milton, stop—"

Rriiippp. He tears the dress from the slit all the way up to the neck, until it's nothing but rags floating to the ground around me.

"What the fuck?" He smiles, and it's oh, so fucking crazy and hot at the same time. Slamming my hands into his chest, he laughs when I push him back just a little. So feeble and pathetic. "You've made your point! I don't want any part in this…this *freakshow*."

"Oh no, you don't." Grabbing me when I try to walk away, he cages me in with his arms. "You don't get to back out now." Reaching around my back, the clasp on my bra loosens as he unclips it. "You wanted to know what it's like to be my girl, and now you will."

"No—" He rips it down my arms and tosses it to the ground before I can grapple to catch it. I can't breathe or think as he does the same to my panties, breaking it at the side and letting it fall down to join the rest of the destroyed pieces of material.

My hands jerk to cover myself, the beginnings of cold panic wrapping around my throat. "Milton—"

"You wanted to play this game, so don't you *dare* move." He shrugs his jacket off. It drops to my feet in a heap, and soon his waistcoat and tie join them. My mouth is bone dry as he reaches for his pants and undoes the button, pulls down the zip, and slowly, almost on purpose, removes them.

My hand trembles as I lift it to move hair from my face, anxious to know how far he's going to take this. The obvious thing that happens in this room is what is taking place behind me, and the thought of Milton doing that to me…now there's a scary thought altogether.

Leaving his shirt and boxers on, he reaches for me. Gripping my ass hard enough to make me cry out, he lifts me until I have no choice but to grab his shoulders and wrap my legs around his torso, so I don't fall.

His skin is fire beneath me as he strides further into the room, my heart skipping a beat when he lifts one of his hands to grab my chin. Pulling me close, his head tilts, and for one gut-turning second, with eyes focused solely on my lips, I think he's going to kiss me.

He doesn't.

Fingers close around my neck, and he's suddenly pushing me back. Terror all but consumes me as water makes contact with my skin. Before I can even see where it's come from, I am completely submerged underwater.

It takes me a moment to realize that Milton is forcing me down in a tub of some sort I didn't see when I first entered this room. Water pours down my ears and up my nose. My lungs burn for the breath I didn't get to take. The fucker stole it before I even hit the water when I thought he was going to kiss me. Like he knew it would.

I thrash out, slapping and hitting him to let go, but he holds me down. That's when real panic kicks in, and I slam my hands into him harder. What I'm hitting, I don't know. What I do know is that he isn't letting go. *Oh, God.*

A frenzy of bubbles spurts from my mouth as I scream. Bad idea. More water rushes in. I'm running out of time. My body is going to be forced to give in. I can feel it.

Maybe I should give in. Finally, die. I can think of worse ways to go. I can be with my baby. I wouldn't have to deal with this exhausting fight any longer. Just let go. Right now.

But then, they win. All the people who set out to ruin me—they all win.

Stop being a victim.

In a last futile attempt, I let my body sag until my back hits the bottom of the tub. Like this, Milton's arm is fully extended down into the water. Dropping my chin and pushing my face forward, I bite down into his arm. Hard.

Blood pools in my mouth as he yanks his arm away, the momentum working in my favor as it drags me up to the surface. Finally, finding purchase with my feet, I break through, coughing and gulping for air.

Blinking water from my eyes, Milton goes to grab me again when something in me takes over. Lashing out with a scream, my hand swipes across his face, leaving red scratches on his cheek. Enough to stun him. I'm knee-deep in a stone bath of water, belonging to what I can only describe as an altar.

"No!" I yell when hands capture my arms.

"No?" he demands, grabbing my face and forcing me to look at him. Blood trickles from the claw marks I left on his skin and the bite on his arm.

"Why did you do that?" I choke on my tears. "Why the fuck are you trying to kill me?"

"Because now you know what it feels like to have someone you care about, someone you would do anything for, try to fucking kill you." His words paralyze me, like I've just been slapped. "*Now* we're even."

My hand connects with the side of his face, and he growls out. Pulling me into him, his lips crash against mine. He kisses me so hard, so *bruising*, it hurts.

But God, am I instantly consumed by him. The feel of his lips. The taste of him. I'm so dizzy from lack of oxygen my limbs are too exhausted to fight him off. And with the way he's kissing me...I'm not sure I even want to.

I can't help but moan into his mouth as he wraps his arms around my waist and draws me out of the tub. Slamming me up against one of the columns nearby, he cups my breasts, thumbs stroking against my hardened nipples. *Oh shit.* The sensation has me groaning louder into his mouth and shuddering from his touch.

Lifting me again, he kisses me harder, grinding his cock between my legs, the fabric of his boxers the only thing between us. He breaks the kiss then, breath shaky as the air hits my lips. I'm in shock, and I think for a moment, he is too. He wasn't meant to kiss me.

Lifting my hand, he catches my wrist before I can touch him, eyes warily searching my face. "Let me touch you," I whisper.

"No." His voice is hoarse. "We're not doing this—"

"Then why allow me to come in here?"

He glares at me, though I'm not sure his anger is directed at me. More himself. "*Humoring* you."

"Bullshit, Milton."

Letting go of my wrist, he pushes my legs apart. Fighting is useless, especially as he inserts two fingers inside my pussy. My world spins, and I moan as he presses his mouth into my ear. "Maybe I do want you…maybe I always have."

"Fuck you. You hated the job Blake gave you." I cry out when he goes even deeper at the mention of Blake's name. "You didn't want to look after me—I was just a burden to you!"

"Still are." He plants me hard against the wall of the column, and I struggle to pay attention to anything other than how his fingers feel inside me. Even with the stone cutting into my spine. Even when he tried to kill me. I'm so achingly wet, needing to find some form of release from this torture he's inflicted on me.

"We can't—" he says, taking his fingers out of me; I whimper in protest.

"No, p-please." I tighten my legs around him, close to tears. "Stop doing this to me."

He gives me a quizzical look. "Doing what?"

"Torturing me." Tears trickle down my face; I'm unable to believe the next words coming out of my mouth. "I want you."

"Fuck sake." He falls into me, lips slamming against mine again. I kiss him back, running my tongue against his lips, the same time reaching to pull the waistband of his boxers down over his length.

Breathing heavily into my mouth, he gives in, lining his cock at my entrance and thrusting inside of me. A breathless cry of shock escapes me as he fills me completely. He trembles when my tongue meets his, and I don't care about all he's done to me. Need is a veracious emotion, and I'm suffocating in it.

Pulling out briefly, he thrusts inside of me. I scream, the pressure in my lower belly growing. He rocks again, sending spirals of fire rippling through me. With both our bodies shaking, he drives into me again and again, his body smacking against mine and shoving my spine into the stone.

"Fuck," he groans into my ear.

Flames and people fucking around us may as well be a dream, because right now, the only two people in this room are him and me. Vision fading, my core ripples, and tightens around his cock.

"Milton," I groan as his hips slam hard into mine, each thrust grinding against my clit. "Ahh!" I yell out, and it only makes him go harder, faster. *Holy shit.*

"Come on, Heidi. Fucking come!" Gripping me tightly, he pumps himself in and out, and just as I think I might pass out, I shatter. My body spasms uncontrollably as he thrusts fiercer, my walls clenching around him feverishly, prolonging my orgasm in a way that steals my breath.

His forehead meets mine, sweaty and hot, and he slows to a stop. I open my eyes just in time to see his face contort with pain as he pulls out of me, and I realize he didn't come.

I want to ask why, but I have no energy. My head falls to the side, and I see others still having sex in the steamy haze. But the edges of my vision darken, and sleep calls me.

CHAPTER TWENTY-FOUR

My eyelids flutter open. I'm back in the bed I was put in the first time I was here, the nice bedroom with its luxurious bed I wonder how many have slept in. As sore as me. As *broken*. Because, like those women, I had sex with the devil.

Seconds. That's all it takes for everything to come rushing back, overwhelming me all at once. I all but scoffed at the mention of Milton running a sex cult in these deep, dark tunnels. How silly. *Ludicrous.* Now, I believe tonight it's exactly what I witnessed. And I participated.

Flipping onto my back, I push the covers off my body, too hot and in pain. My back and between my legs are sore, but the sickness inside of me likes it—throbs for more. One time wasn't enough.

After tonight, I know I'm as deep in Milton's inferno as I'm ever going to be, and I need to know what's to happen now. I have to know how far this is going to go…and if he still plans on sending me away.

Taking my time climbing out of bed, I go over to the door and pull it open, I start down the hall toward the living room, my insides sinking with disappointment when I don't find Milton on the couch.

Just as I think he might not be here at all, a noise coming from a direction I've never been before have me curiously stepping forward. Slowly passing a small kitchenette adjoining the living area, I turn a corner, spotting two double black doors at the end of another corridor. Edging nearer, the sound of metal clinking together dries my mouth as I put my hand on the cold handle.

Cracking it open, just enough to see inside, my lips part when Milton's naked, toned chest confronts me. His upper body is on display as he leans back against a workout bench. Heavy breaths fill the air as he pushes weights, muscles contorting, and bulging every time he strains. As I watch the beads of moisture roll across his body, I bite down on my lip, wincing when I break skin and taste blood.

Grunting, he drops the weights back down on the bar and sits up, grabbing a towel to wipe his face. Turning in my direction, he stops when he sees me spying on him by the door, almost as if he could sense me there. Like I know when he is.

I go still, taking in his face, his flushed cheeks. The way his hair clings to his forehead, eyes so troubled I wish I knew why. I don't move as he walks over to me, soon stopping in front of me.

"I'm..." He suddenly reaches out and grabs me, pulling me inside. Pain shoots up my already sore spine as he slams me up against the door, lips meeting mine and stealing me of my breath. My life. My fucking soul.

Wrapping my fingers around his neck, I arch my back to deepen the kiss. He groans, his tongue frantically tearing past my lips and touching mine. Tasting me as much as I am him. We kiss like that for a while. Slow and hard and so fucking good. Grabbing the backs of my knees, he lifts me and wraps my legs around his waist. I cling to him as he kisses along my jaw and down my neck, his erection pressing against me. My stomach loops and curls as I grasp his hair and clench my fist, rewarded as he inhales sharply against my neck.

"What do you want?" I ask, his nipples peaking as I run my hands over his body, his muscles quivering under my fingertips.

"I want a lot of things." He leans in to kiss down my throat.

"Tell me."

He pulls away, still clinging onto me. Gritting his teeth. "*You*, and that's something you wouldn't want to happen. Not ever."

"Why?"

He doesn't answer right away, and I'm only more confused when he does. "Because I will fuck you up more than you already are."

He grabs the straps of the black nightdress he must have dressed me in and pulls them down over my arms. My breasts fall free, and I whimper when he cups them, thumbs grazing my nipples, adding enough pressure for me to feel it between my legs.

"You would finally understand the real meaning of ownership. I wouldn't just own you. You would need me like your next breath. Crave me like the purest drug." His teeth nip at my neck, punctuating each sentence. "And you would own me." As if only just figuring it out himself, he releases me and takes a step back. His hands run through his hair in frustration. "This shouldn't have ever happened."

Bitterness crawls inside of me like a disease and a frown creases his forehead from my expression. At my disappointment. The fire is back in his eyes, and he reaches to grab me again. But this time, I pull away.

"You tell me to stop playing the victim...then stop treating me like one." I touch his chest and push him back, forcing him to sit on the bench. He watches me warily as I kneel in front of him and grab his black shorts, but he slaps my hand away, hard enough to sting.

"No," he says. "I won't take pleasure from you."

I reach for him again. My fingers brushing against his rigid length as I pull the strings loose. His teeth clench together like he's in pain.

"God damn it, stop." He catches my wrists, but I pull away from him and look down, seeing a pair of black briefs cupping his erection. I stroke him through the fabric, and he flinches. Grabbing my shoulders, he glares down at me. "Can't you see I don't fucking want you? Go back to bed."

Humiliation burns through me, like a bucket of ice being thrown over me. But it's not true. I know it's not. "You *do* want me."

His hands shake as he squeezes my skin, blunt nails digging into me. But I ignore the pain and pull the elastic waist of his briefs downward, enough to free his cock that springs forward, solid with moisture glistening at the tip.

My mouth pools. I've never *wanted* to put someone in my mouth before. The sight of him quaking at my touch turns me on and I'm dying to taste him.

I *want* to own him.

Once again, he grabs my wrists and forces them to my side. "I will hurt you. Don't."

"You won't."

"The last time I saw you like this, you were sucking that fucker's cock."

My eyes squint. "And I bet you wished it was yours."

"Fuck you, Heidi," he spits, and I lean forward, licking his tip, tasting him. Oh, fuck. He tastes so good, and I wrap my mouth around his thick knob, stretching my jaw to take more of him into my mouth. He suddenly grabs my hair and yanks my head back. He looks menacing. Like he wants to kill me for real this time. "You have no idea how close I was to gunning everyone in that room down that night. I wanted to. And the way you sucked him off—"

"You think I *liked* it?"

"Yes." I lay my hands on his thighs and drag my nails down his skin, tearing into his flesh but only leaving marks.

"I did what I had to do, unlike *you*."

Despite him still having hold of my hair, I lean forward and lick him again, never wanting something so badly in my life. To taste him and fuck him with my mouth. He was right—I do crave him. I did back then, and I do right now.

I lift my eyes in time to see torture spreading over his face as he watches me take him into my mouth again. How I slide my tongue down his long length, lapping him up before sucking. "Does it feel good?"

I dig my nails in harder as he tries to stand, this time feeling his skin break under my fingers. His breaths get heavier. "Stop. For fuck sake, stop."

I open wider, wrapping him with my mouth and move my head down until he's hitting the back of my throat. I don't stop, and every time I take a tiny peek, his eyes are intense. Angry. Insane for me.

Then, as if something in him snaps, he grabs me, forcing my mouth away from him. Instead of pushing me away like I think he will, he lifts and turns me until I'm sitting reclined on the bench, my head perfectly aligned with his jutting member.

Grabbing my hair to keep me in place, he presses his cock to my lips and shoves himself back inside my mouth.

"Is this what you wanted?" He sounds angry as his hips propel, forcing me to take him deeper, his accent more profound again. My eyes water, but I take all of him, his moan like music to my ears. Even though my throat is burning, and it feels like my jaw might snap in two, I don't want him to stop. "For me to fuck your beautiful mouth like this?"

Pulling out and pushing in, I force myself to relax. To take him. I want to take him. To prove to him.

"You think just because I fucked you, I *want* you?" He lurches down my throat again, fingers wrapping around my neck, blocking my air. He's choking me as he fucks my mouth. Hard. Fast. Never-ending. My throat cries out in protest, lungs ablaze.

Grabbing his wrists, I squeeze my eyes shut, and just as I think I might pass out, he comes loudly, roaring out as his cock pulsates against my tongue, cum splashing down the back of my throat. I swallow down every drop he empties inside of me. Until he pulls free, releasing my neck. I tilt forward with the momentum, gasping for air as I fall on my hands and knees.

There's a bang. Milton rips through the room, breaking furniture and smashing everything he can get his hands on. Gasping when I'm almost hit by a piece of apparatus, I crawl backward, until my back hits the wall. It feels like my throat has been split open. I reach up when something dribbles down my chin. After touching whatever it is, I'm shocked when blood coats my fingers. Right now, there's no way to tell if it's come from him or me.

He thunders through the room and smashes his fists into everything he can. Splitting open his skin and making himself bleed. Then, he turns to me, his chest heaving up and down, eyes clouded with a mixture of emotions that I'm not able to decipher. Just one.

Hate.

My bottom lip trembles as he storms over and grabs me. Opening the door, he pushes me out into the hall, yelling, "Get out!"

Reaching for the straps of my nightdress, I cover myself, a sob breaking through my lips. "W-Why?"

He slams the door in my face without saying anything more, and I move back when he yells out, his fists colliding with the door. Every thunderous bang pushes me further away. Until Milton's destruction resorts me to breaking down and crying.

Continuing to shuffle back, the door getting further and further away, I'm stopped when my back hits a pair of legs.

"Get up." A voice I swear I know snarls. Looking behind me, expensive polished shoes that belong to a man are right next to me. Craning my neck, I glance upward, sucking in a breath when I see Milton's friend. Maxim Koslov.

He's standing above me, black eyes glaring at me with disgust. Anger. "I *said*, get up."

I swallow nervously as I stand. Wearing a gray suit with a red tie, his steely cold eyes connect with mine before snapping to the room Milton is still wrecking.

I'm not sure what crosses his mind, though I get the feeling Milton's outburst has perturbed him. And it's clear as he puts his gaze back on me where he's pointing the blame. But then, I am to blame. "Come with me."

"I-I can't." I try to go back to Milton, to stop him, but Maxim grabs my arm and tugs me forward. I yelp, his grip like a vice. "You're hurting—"

"You'd be wise to not disobey me," he warns, tone dripping with so much darkness, I shudder. "I'm not opposed to giving a woman a good slap when needed."

He drags me away, and he isn't gentle about it. Throwing me onto one of the couches, he roars, "Lisa!" Coming from nowhere and stumbling in her heels, it's obvious even Lisa is afraid of Maxim as he barks out, "*YA khochu kontrakt Milton s etoy devushkoy.*"

She pulls a piece of paper from her bag promptly, and when he grabs it from her, he turns to me. "You see this?" It's the contract —the one I only signed tonight.

He rips it. Right down the middle. Until it's nothing but pieces floating to the ground.

"*Idti k nemu,*" he says in an ordering tone. Nodding, Lisa goes in the direction we left. To Milton.

"In five minutes, you are getting in a car, and it will take you back to whatever hole you crawled out of."

My heart drops to my stomach. No. He can't do this. "I can't leave—"

"I don't want to see your face in this place again. Do you understand?" he demands, and the realization of what he's doing sinks in. That he's taking me away from Milton. Emotion clogs in my throat, and I start sobbing. He tuts. "Crying won't get you anywhere with me."

"You don't understand—"

He pins me with a murderous stare. "Oh, I understand perfectly, *suka*. Whatever's been going on between you and Milton ends tonight."

"No," I shout, despite the fear of this man. "I can't leave him. He's protecting me!"

"Not anymore."

Grabbing me, he pulls me off the couch and marches me all the way to the entrance of the mansion, not caring that I'm shoeless, only wearing a nightdress and have blood down my chin. Not caring as I weep and plead for him to return me to Milton.

A car screeches around the drive, coming to a stop right in front of us. The man I remember to be Lucius gets out of the driver's seat and opens the back door. Thrusting me forward, Maxim tries to push me into the car. "No!"

Attempting to run back inside is futile with a grip like Maxim's. Slamming me up against the side of the car, he takes my wrist and glares down at my hand. My eyes drop. He's looking at the ring. "You won't be needing *this* anymore."

Ripping it off my finger, I cry harder. "Please stop."

He pushes me inside the car and slams the door in my face. Lucius is already in the driver's seat and speeding away.

"It's for the best," I hear him say as tears fall like rivulets down my face.

"Shut up!" I kick his back seat. They don't get it. Not that it bothers Lucius. He keeps driving until all I can do is fall against the seat and cry some more.

Breaking, breaking. Destroyed.

Milton's reaction plays in my mind as we travel. I'm not sure where I went wrong, but what I do know is that I pushed him to the brink and I got more than just a glimpse into his world. His demons screamed, and mine called back. And leaving him now only makes me realize how much I do need him. How I need more than just his protection.

But in Fair Haven, things like that come with a price, and having Milton may just cost me everything.

~ Continues in Reign ~

ABOUT THE AUTHOR

Living in the hills of Ireland and spending years writing books online, Lydia's dream has always been to one day become a published author. When she isn't escaping into the many worlds inside her head, she's a devoted mother to three beautiful children and partner.

https://authorlydiagoodfellow.com

ALSO BY LYDIA GOODFELLOW

Club XXX
Worship
Reign

Printed in Poland
by Amazon Fulfillment
Poland Sp. z o.o., Wrocław